Contents...series 1.

Page 3 **Zombie and Sarge...the beginning.** S1E1

Page 26 **The Village Fete.** S1E2

Page 33 **The Great Zombini.** S1E3

Page 47 **Sarge's Birthday.** S1E4

Page 59 **Zombie and the Football Fans.** S1E5

Page 70 **Zombie and Zombier.** S1E6

Page 82 **The Award Ceremony.** S1E7

Page 95 **Zombie and the Kittens.** S1E8

Page 108 **Zombie and the Holiday.** S1E9

Page 128 **Zombie goes to Therapy.** S1E10

Page 142 **Zombie turns to Crime.** S1E11

Page 162 **Zombie's Hard Work.** S1E12

Page 203 **Zombie's Hard Work – rap.** S1E12a

Zombie and Sarge – The Beginning   S1E1

Narrator:

Sarge - is a career policeman in charge of a very small village police station. He's a terse, no-nonsense type with a short temper.

Zombie – created by top-brass in a hush-hush experiment is an idiot. Lovable – but an idiot, nonetheless.

The Meeting:

Chief Inspector: Ah, Spicer… glad you could make it. It's through here.

Narrator: Spicer is led to a morgue with a figure covered in a sheet. The sheet is lifted, and the figure is hooked up to wires and machinery.

Sarge: A d…d…dead body Chief Inspector?

Chief Inspector: A zombie to be more precise.

Sarge: A z...z... a zombie?!?

Chief Inspector: Keep your voice down! Yes, our latest secret weapon in the fight against crime. What with budget cuts etc, we've had to be more 'creative' in our recruitment drive. So, the boffins created 'Zombie'. Low maintenance, easy to control and low on intelligence.

Sarge: He'll make a perfect copper then...

Chief Inspector: Exactly! And because he's only an experiment, we decided to test him out on a small nick with low crime rates that mainly deals with paperwork. That's why... we're giving him to you to train up.

Sarge: But, but... I don't want a new recruit! Especially... a zombie!

Chief Inspector: Nonsense. You've always complained about how much time paperwork takes. Yes, you'll have to teach him how to act human, but I have every faith in you. We'll give it six months and take it from there. Right, stand back, let's activate him.

Narrator: A lever is pulled. Electricity crackles and Zombie slowly rises...Zombie groggily wakes up. A stupid, broad grin on his face

Zombie: Hello, my name is Zombie. Pleased to meet you. What are you doing in my bedroom???

Sarge: This is not your bedroom you idiot! This is a morgue.

Zombie: I thought it was a bit cold.

Chief Inspector: We'll get him dressed, and after a debrief, you can take him back to the nick to get him accustomed to his new life in the outside world. And Spicer, don't forget, this is a hush-hush experiment, so we've arranged a cover story that he's a new recruit you're training. If you are successful, there could be promotion in it...

Narrator: Zombie is dressed in uniform, debriefed, and drives off with Sarge.

Sarge: Right Zombie, let's get a few things straight before we start.

Zombie: Right you are Sarge. I'll start right away.

Sarge: Zombie, why have you lined up all my pens and pencils??

Zombie: You said let's get a few things straight.

Narrator: Sarge - slightly irritated but trying to remain calm.

Sarge: When we say, 'get things straight', us humans mean 'to make things clear'. So, to make things clear, I run this place. You don't do anything unless I tell you to. Understood?

Zombie: Yes Sarge.

Sarge: Good. Right, this big desk is mine. You don't touch anything on it, not the computer, not the phone, not the pens and paper not even a paper clip, understand?

Zombie: Yes Sir!

Sarge: But don't worry, you get that little desk in the corner.

Zombie: Got it Sarge, now what should I do with it?

Sarge: Put the desk down Zombie! When I said you *get* it, I mean - that's where you work. Now, if you are very good and don't do any more stupid things, you might even get some pens and paper. You'd like that, wouldn't you Zombie?

Zombie: Ooh goody goody. Yes Sarge. And can I have some of those pink things too?

Sarge: Hehe, those are called post it notes. Yes, you can... only if you're good mind. Now, let's show you how to make a cup of tea... you'll mainly be in charge of that... and we drink a lot of tea here you'll find. Now, *this* thing is called a kettle and once we've filled it up with water, we press *this* button to boil the water and pour it on top of the bags which we put into *these* things called cups and add milk and sugar. Do you think you can do that whilst I check my phone messages?

Zombie: Yes Sarge.

Narrator: A short while later...

Sarge: Zombie... why is there a plastic bag in my cup?!

Zombie: You said pour hot water onto the bag.

Narrator: Sarge - trying to keep calm but letting out a growl.

Sarge: I meant TEABAG! Look... one of *these*.

Zombie: Owww...

Sarge: Never mind, forget the tea. I'll show you around the nick. You've already seen the front desk area and the kitchen. The bathroom is this room here, and down this corridor is the cells where we keep any prisoners, we are processing.

Zombie: Ooh ooh, can I see the prisoners?

Sarge: Hehe, there are no prisoners, we rarely have any here, but I'll tell you what...go and take the big key hanging up in that cabinet, and you can open the cell door.

Zombie: Ooh goody goody.

Sarge: I'm going to go to the loo while you do that.

Narrator: Zombie calls to Sarge from the cell.

Zombie: And what do I do with the key after?

Narrator: Sarge replies from the bathroom.

Sarge: If there's someone in the cell, hang it back up, but when there's nobody in the cell, you keep it on you.

That way, when the cell door locks, we can unlock it from the inside.

Zombie: Ooh it is very cold in here... and a bit dark...

Narrator: Sarge rejoins Zombie in the cell.

Sarge: Yes, they're not built for comfort. There's the bunk bed, sink and basic loo and that's it. And once this door is shut - like *this*... the prisoners can't get out - unless we let them out.

Zombie: Let them out?

Sarge: Yes, yes, let them out.

Zombie: How?

Sarge: How?? With the key of course.

Zombie: The key?

Sarge: Yes, yes, the key, the key Zombie.

Zombie: What, the key I unlocked the door with? The one you said put back if there is someone in the cell?

Sarge: Yes, yes Zombie. The one you keep on you if the cell is empty.

Zombie: Don't you worry Sarge, it's nice and safe!

Sarge: Good, that's what I like to see, a security-minded policeman. Right, give me the key and I'll show you our sleeping quarters. They are more comfortable than a night in this cell with just a thin blanket.

Zombie: I can't give you the key Sarge, I hung it up in the cabinet...

Sarge: You half-wit!! I said to only put the key away if there was someone **in** the cell!!

Zombie: There was someone in the cell when you said that, **I** was in here...

Sarge: I meant prisoners you idiot! Now we've got to spend the night in the cells, until the cleaner comes in in the morning...

Zombie: Never mind, we can play a game to pass the time. I spy with my little eye, something beginning with B...

Sarge: Bloody idiot!

Zombie: That's two words.

Sarge: I was describing you, you bloody idiot!

Zombie: No that would be Z, Z for Zombie. Try again.

Sarge: No thank you Zombie. I don't want to play a game, and quite frankly, don't want to hear you speak again!

Zombie: It was bars, B for bars.

Sarge: Quiet Zombie. Let's get some sleep instead.

Zombie: But I'm wide awake. I know, let's sing a song. 'I know a song that will really get on your nerves, really get on your nerves, really…'

Sarge: Zombie shut up!!... Please.

Zombie: Ooer, there's no need to shout.

Sarge: Hmmn. Right, I'm sorry. But the best thing to do is sleep till the morning. Besides, the lights automatically go out soon, so we'll have to sleep. Right about… now… in fact.

Zombie: Ooh, it's gone a bit dark. W…w… where are you Sarge??

Sarge: I'm in bed. I suggest you get in bed too.

Zombie: Right you are Sarge. Sarge?

Sarge: Yes Zombie?

Zombie: Do you think the moon is made out of cheese?

Sarge: Don't be so bloody stupid, of course not!

Zombie: Sarge, how many blades of grass do you think there are in the world?

Sarge: Zombie – SHUT UP!

Zombie: Well, there's no need to shout...

Sarge: Listen Zombie, if you promise to be quiet, I PROMISE to give you some of those pink post-it notes. You'd like that, wouldn't you Zombie?

Zombie: Ooh goody goody, can I have three of them?

Sarge: You can have five... if you PROMISE To be quiet for the rest of the night...

Zombie: I hope you're not trying to bribe a police officer?!

Sarge: Hmmmn. Of course not, now is it a deal?

Zombie: Yes Sarge!

Sarge: Good. Now, just one more thing...

Zombie: What's that Sarge?

Sarge: Could you get out of my bunk and into your own bed!? There's a good lad!

Narrator: The next morning, the cleaner unlocks the cell door and discovers Sarge and Zombie.

Mrs. Buckle: Ere, what you doing in here? You narf give me a turn!

Sarge: What's going on? Where am I??

Mrs Buckle: You are sleeping in the cells which I've come in to clean. What you doing in here it's not like you not to be in the comfort of your sleeping quarters Mr Spicer? Ere, you didn't lock yourself in did you?

Sarge: Lock myself in? How preposterous! Only an idiot would do that Mrs Buckle. No no, I was erm, showing our new recruit what it would be like to be a prisoner. You know, put yourself in their shoes - so to speak... as well as giving him the confidence of how secure the cells are.

Mrs Buckle: There's two of you in here??

Narrator: Zombie leans down from the top bunk grinning away.

Zombie: Morning Mrs Bucket, I'm Zombie. Pleased to meet you.

Mrs Buckle: Zombie you say? Well, you look like death warmed up.

Zombie: Funny you should say that, because yesterday I WAS dead!

Sarge: Dead on his feet he means Mrs Bucket... I mean Mrs Buckle, dead on his feet as he had a very busy day.

Zombie: No, I actually WAS...

Narrator: Sarge muffles Zombie's mouth with his hand.

Sarge: That's enough PC Zombie, Mrs Buckle is a busy lady and hasn't got time for your ramblings. Now, let's leave her to it and get ready for today's shift. I'll show you around the village once PC Smith arrives to take over desk duties.

Narrator: A while later PC Smith arrives...

Sarge: Ah Smith, this is PC Zombie a new recruit HQ have tasked me with training up. I'm going to show him our local patch, so you'll be on desk duty till I return.

PC Smith: Righto Sarge.

Narrator: Smith mans the police station and Sarge takes Zombie on their beat.

Sarge: Right, the route we normally take is marked on this map here, which I'll let you keep after I've shown you, so you don't get lost.

Zombie: Right you are Sarge.

Sarge: So, we start from the police station, which is marked here on the map. Then we go down the High Street where there is the bank, the garage, the supermarket and the pub. Then there's the butchers, the bakers and...

Zombie: ...the candlestick makers?

Sarge: And the candlestick... no no don't be silly, the grocer's. Then at the end is the post office. Once we've done the High Street, we come back along this route here past the hospital, through the park...

Zombie: Ooh goody goody, can we go on the swings?

Sarge: No!

Zombie: Owww.

Sarge: Then once you come out of the park you go past the sweet shop...

Zombie: ...can we...?

Sarge: No! Then past the antique shop, doctors then back here. Now I might have missed out some of the shops, but you get the idea - that we go in a big loop. Got that?

Zombie: Yes Sarge. I leave the police station. Go loopy. Then come back!

Sarge: Zombie, I'm about to lose my patience.

Zombie: Don't worry Sarge, we'll find them at the hospital.

Narrator: Sarge growls but tries to be calm…

Sarge: Just… just come with me on our beat.

Zombie: Right you are Sarge.

Sarge: Right, this is the bank. We'll pop in so you'll need a mask.

Zombie: Oh no Sarge, I don't think we should rob it – we're the police!

Sarge: Eh? Oh, I see. Ah yes… I forgot to tell you while you were aslee…being crea… before you were, before you were…

Zombie: Born?

Sarge: Ah yes born. There was a pandemic and everyone had to wear a mask and keep 2 metres apart. Although restrictions are nearly lifted now, we still must keep 2 metres apart and wear a face covering.

Zombie: Right you are Sarge.

Sarge: ...OK that's the bank done. Now, I'll walk with you halfway down the High Street, then you can do the rest of the route on your own, so I can go back to the station to catch up on some slee...I mean paperwork! Of course, if there is a problem, you can get hold of me on the police radio.

Zombie: Right you are Sarge.

Sarge: OK, this is where I'll leave you. Now, you've got the map of the route and if you need me at all for any help or advice, call me up on the radio.

Narrator: Zombie starts talking to himself...

Zombie: You've got this Zombie, you can do this Zombie, you can do policemanning.

Woman: Help! Stop that man, he stole my purse!

Zombie: Don't worry woman on the street, policeman Zombie will catch him. Where did he go?

Woman: There, down that alley.

Narrator: Zombie runs down the alley…

Zombie: Aha! A dead end. I'm policeman Zombie, and you're nicked.

Thief: Look, you can have the purse, but you can't touch me. Catch!

Zombie: There you go Madam, there's your purse back, now leave him to me.

Woman: Oh, thank you so much officer. Goodbye.

Zombie: Now, what do you mean I can't touch you?

Thief: You've got to socially distance by keeping 2 metres apart.

Zombie: Oh yes that's right, Sarge told me about that. Well, how am I going to arrest you then??

Thief: Well, since I threw you the purse, you throw me the handcuffs and I'll put them on.

Zombie: Good idea, here you are. Catch!

Thief: Hur hur, cheers. Ere, I can't work out how these go on.

Zombie: Oh come on, even an idiot could work out how to put them on. Throw them over here, and I'll show you.

Thief: Righto… there you go.

Zombie: Now watch carefully. Now, you take the cuffs like this and put one side on the pole as if it was your wrist… like this.

Thief: Yeah, but that's a pole you've put one end on, that doesn't show me how they go on a wrist.

Zombie: Alright I'll put the other end on my wrist like this… Now, you just stay there whilst I find the key to unlock myself.

Thief: You must have been born yesterday if you think I'm going to hang around. See you officer, hur hur.

Zombie: How did **you** know I was born yesterday? Here, hold on don't run away, I haven't found the key yet. Got it. Oh darn, I dropped it down the drain. I'd better radio Sarge. He's going to be so cross. "Zombie calling Sarge, Zombie calling Sarge, do you read me?" "Over".

Sarge: This is Sergeant Spicer Zombie, what is the matter? Aha… yes…purse… trapped the thief in an alley yes… social distancing… good… got purse back - very good…made an arrest… excellent… but you arrested YOURSELF!! You idiot… lost the key down the drain and can I come and rescue you? I should leave you there, but I'll be there straight away...

Zombie: Cooee Sarge, I'm over here, handcuffed to his pole. I can't unlock myself because the key is down that drain.

Sarge: You're a complete idiot Zombie!

Zombie: Thank you very much Sarge.

Sarge: That wasn't a compliment Zombie!

Zombie: Yes it was. Because yesterday - I was only a half-wit.

Sarge: Hmmmn. Anyway, now I've got to put my hand down this smelly drain. Yuck! Right, got the key, now once I've freed you, I'm going to have to go back to the nick and clean up. You carry on to the park then head back. And Zombie, keep an eye out for that thief - I want him caught!

Zombie: Right you are Sarge.

Narrator: At the park...

Boy: Policeman, I want Fifi. Boohoohoo.

Zombie: Why didn't you go before you came out?

Boy: Wah haa haa! I want Fifi!

Zombie: OK little boy, no need to cry. Come with me and we'll find out where the loo is.

Old lady: Oh well done Timmy you found a policeman to help find my dog.

Zombie: Oh, Fifi is a dog.

Old lady: Yes, Foo Foo here is her twin brother, aren't you my little Foo Foo woo foo?

Narrator: The dog barks and yaps excitedly making a nuisance of himself.

Old lady: Quiet Foo Foo, I'm trying to talk to the officer, you'll knock us over if you carry on.

Zombie: So, what happened Madam?

Old lady: Well, my grandson and I were walking along when he slipped on some...

Narrator: The dog barks loudly whilst the old lady is trying to talk...

Old lady: Shh Foo Foo, I'm trying to talk to this policeman. Sorry about that. As I was saying, Timmy slipped on some leaves and let go of Fifi and she ran into that bushy area. But it's too dense for us to go in.

Zombie: Nothing is too dense for me for me, don't you worry.

Old lady: She might come out if you throw her a stick. Foo Foo stop getting under everyone's feet.

Narrator: Foo Foo gives out a yelp and runs off after Zombie treads on him.

Old lady: You trod on my Foo Foo, now he's also run off. Now what are you going to do??

Zombie: I'd better ring Sarge…

Sarge: …Yes, this is Sarge Zombie. In the park yes… you trod on what?? Now you want to know if you should use a stick to get it out?? Stay right where you are Zombie. I'm coming!

Old lady: Oh, here comes my doggies now, running after that man. I must thank him when he reaches us.

Zombie: And here comes Sarge.

Sarge: Right, what's been going on?

Old lady: Oh, everything is alright now officer. My doggies had run off, but your constable was trying to help, when that man - walking away, lured them out of the bushes. Could you thank him for me whilst I make sure my babies are OK?

Sarge: You heard the lady Zombie, go and thank the man.

Zombie: Right you are Sarge.

Sarge: Why have you bought him back in handcuffs Zombie, you were meant to thank him, not arrest him! I'm sorry about this Sir.

Zombie: No Sarge, this is the purse snatcher who forgot to be arrested earlier. He was hiding from us in those bushes when Fifi and Foo Foo found him.

Sarge: Oh, what good work Zombie! Well Madam, I'll leave you to enjoy the rest of the day with your dogs and grandson whilst we take this little oik to the nick. Good day.

Zombie: Saaaaarge...

Sarge: What is it PC Zombie?

Zombie: Can we get an ice crea...

Sarge: No!

Zombie: Owww

Sarge: But I will say, it's been a perfect end to a trying morning.

Zombie: I wouldn't speak too soon Sarge...

Sarge: Why not? We caught this one and rescued a couple of dogs for an old lady.

Zombie: But take a look at your trouser leg Sarge... I think Foo Foo has had a Fifi on it.

Sarge: Baaah!

The Village Fete   S1E2

Narrator: It's the day of the village fete and Sarge is looking forward to entering his prize vegetables into the local growers' competition.

Sarge: Ah, Zombie there you are, how's your vegetable growing going? Think you might win any prizes? Pah ha ha.

Zombie: I'm going to enter myself!

Sarge: You can't enter yourself into a fruit and veg competition!!

Zombie: Yes I can! Or why would you keep calling me a prize banana otherwise then?

Sarge: Hmmn...Anyway, humans can't be entered, only fruit and veg - like this great big marrow that I have grown.

Zombie: Wow, that's really big! That must have taken ages to grow...

Sarge: Yes, it took months and months of painstaking loving care and attention to grow it to this size.

Zombie: Ooh, I hope you win. All I managed to grow was this black grape.

Sarge: That's not a grape you fool, it's an olive! Mind you, Mr McGurk who judges the competition, is so short-sighted, he'd probably think it WAS a grape.

Zombie: Oh darn, I've just dropped it down the drain... owww.

Sarge: Never mind Zombie, you can enter this cabbage I've grown. You never know, you might win something. He he he.

Zombie: Cheers Sarge.

Sarge: And Zombie, when we get there, I want you on your best behaviour as I'm very respected in the community.

Narrator: At the village fete...

Sarge: Ah Mr McGurk, I assume you're judging the growers' competition again?

Mr McGurk: I am indeed Sergeant Spicer, are you entering this melon?

Sarge: It's a marrow!!

Mr McGurk: Oh, I must need better glasses... you do know a slug has crawled off the marrow onto your face?

Sarge: That's my moustache!

Mr McGurk: And is this your son? Hasn't he grown!

Sarge: No, he's not my son, this is PC Zombie - a new recruit.

Mr McGurk: Pleased to meet you PC Zombie.

Zombie: Just call me Zombie Mr Gerkin.

Sarge: Hehehe. Right Zombie, I'm going to meet all my Neighbourhood Watch friends, you take my marrow for me, would you?

Zombie: Right you are Sarge. 'scuse me Mr Gerkin, where do I put these vegetables?

Mr McGurk: What have you got?

Zombie: A lovely cabbage and Sarge's rotten old marrow.

Mr McGurk: Rotten stuff goes in that pile ready for the pigs and your lovely cabbage on this table.

Narrator: Meanwhile, elsewhere at the fete…

Sarge: Ah, Mrs Polka, still making your marvellous jam?

Mrs Polka: I am indeed Mr Spicer… I am indeed.

Sarge: And Mr. Hill, how's your farm? Did you bring your pigs to eat the spoiled fruit and veg?

Mr. Hill: Indeed, I did Sergeant Spicer... and they'll be having their tea soon, just before they do the judging.

Narrator: Zombie has dealt with the veg and is now looking for Sarge.

Zombie: There you are Sarge. Mr Gerkin said they're about to judge the veg...

Sarge: Oh good... what table did you put my marrow on?

Zombie: Table?

Sarge: Yes Zombie – table. You... did... put it on... one of the tables... didn't you?

Zombie: No! Mr Gerkin told me to put any rotten fruit or veg in that pile over there...

Sarge: I'm not even going to ask...But, just to make sure... you put my marrow and your cabbage on that pile - that is being fed to the pigs?

Zombie: No, no, no... my cabbage is on that table with those really tiny cabbages.

Sarge: And...my lovely marrow??

Zombie: That rotten old thing is in that pile that the pigs are about to eat...you'd better hurry 'cos you might be too late.

Narrator: Sarge heads over to the pig pen and climbs in...

Sarge: Uughh, this is so smelly... good piggies, let me just get that marrow you're about to eat...

Narrator: Sarge slips and slides everywhere, and the pigs have eaten most of the marrow by the time he gets up.

Zombie: Oh dear Sarge, you seem to be covered in pig...

Sarge: Shh Zombie, as I'm about to kill you!!

Narrator: A voice over the tannoy announces: "Will all entrants please make their way to the main marquee as the judging is about to begin."

Zombie: I better go Sarge, I want to see how my cabbage does...

Sarge: Get back here Zombie, I haven't finished with you...Zombie... ZOMBIE! You... wait... till... I get you...

Narrator: Zombie ducks into the marquee just in time for Mr McGerk to announce Zombie as the winner.

Mr McGurk: First prize goes to Mr Zombie. I've never seen such a prize sprout in my life. Here's your gold rosette and the Winners' Cup.

Zombie: It's not a sprout it's a...

Narrator: Zombie is interrupted by the muck covered figure of Sarge standing in the entrance to the marquee.

Sarge: There... you... are!

Mr McGurk: By golly, what's that 'thing' standing in the doorway?

Mrs Polka: I don't know, but it's clutching an armful of rotten fruit and veg and absolutely smells. Poowee!

Mr. Hill: And it's coming this way! Run everybody!

Narrator: Everybody scatters as Sarge overturns tables to get at Zombie and start throwing rotten veg at him.

Sarge: Give... me... that... cup! It's mine I tell you... come here I say...

Narrator: Zombie is chased all the way back to the police station by an angry Sarge... all you can hear is a: "Ooh hoo hoo hoo" fading into the distance...

The Great Zombini   S1E3

Narrator: Sarge is practising for the talent show that the village put on every year. His show is a mixture of magic, jokes and balloon modelling. Zombie is watching...

Sarge: Ladies and Gentlemen, I am the great Marvello, you will be amazed by my magic, tickled by my jokes and amused by my balloon creations. Can I ask a for a volunteer from the audience please?

Zombie: I'll do it Sarge.

Sarge: Hmmn, well you can help me for now because there's no one at the station, but next Saturday, I'll be using a member of the audience.

Zombie: Owww, why can't I be your assistant?

Sarge: Because Zombie, a real human is less likely to make things go wrong.

Zombie: I could do my own magic show instead then!

Sarge: Pah! You couldn't possibly do magic like me; I've been practising for years.

Zombie: If you showed me how to... I could.

Sarge: Somehow, I doubt it Zombie, you're not bright enough.

Zombie: I'll have you know I'm really clever.

Sarge: As clever as a potato. Anyway, OK… this trick requires you to keep an eye on the cup I put the ball under and point to the one it's under when I finish moving them around. Got it?

Zombie: It's under that one!

Sarge: You have to wait for me to move them round like… this.

Narrator: Sarge shifts the cups around

Zombie: That one!

Sarge: Hehe, no.

Zombie: That one?

Sarge: Hehe. Nope. See Zombie, not as easy as it looks, is it? Here, let me show you a card trick. Pick any card from the pack and show the audience.

Zombie: I can't.

Sarge: Why not?

Zombie: There is not an audience.

Sarge: Hmmn, just imagine there is, so they know what card you picked.

Zombie: Oh, I see. I picked the three of diamonds everybody.

Sarge: Grrr! You're meant to keep it to yourself Zombie. Give it here!

Zombie: Make up your mind, do you want the card back or am I keeping it to myself??

Sarge: Let's try again, shall we? Pick a card, look at it… without telling me, and put it back in the pack when you've memorised what card you've picked.

Zombie: OK done it.

Sarge: OK I will now shuffle the cards and your card will end up on the top…was **this** your card - the seven of clubs?

Zombie: Wow, that's amazing! Yes it was the seven of clubs!

Sarge: And I make balloon animals in my act. Like…this giraffe… here…

Zombie: Ooh, ooh, can I keep it Sarge?

Sarge: I suppose so. And I end my show by escaping from locks and handcuffs. Do you want to see?

Zombie: Ooh, goody goody. Yes please!

Sarge: OK, first I put on these special handcuffs. Then... you throw that blanket over me and wrap that chain around tight and padlock it.

Zombie: Done.

Sarge: Now, you set off that big timer on the desk and I will escape before all the sand runs out.

Zombie: On your marks... get set... GO.

Narrator: Sarge moves around under the blanket for a while...

Sarge: Tada! I've escaped!

Zombie: Wow, that's amazing how do you do it??

Sarge: Ah, a magician never reveals his secrets, but I'll just say, I have to have my special handcuffs, it can't be done with regular ones. Yes, the audience love my shows. I've represented the police for the past five talent shows I'll have you know.

Zombie: Sarge, can I represent the police this year and do the magic show? Please, please, please go on...

Sarge: No, no, no, no, no Zombie. You'd ruin it. You don't even know how to do the cup trick.

Zombie: Yes I do, let me get some plastic beakers out of the cupboard and I'll show you...

Sarge: Hmmn...

Zombie: Ladies and Gentlemen, I am the Great Zombini, and I'm going to amaze you by making this ball disappear underneath these cups. Can I have a volunteer to help me? You Sir, what's your name?

Sarge: It's Sarge Zombie, you know that!

Zombie: OK Sarge Zombie, I'm going to hide this ball under one of these cups, switch them around and you've got to guess which one, OK? Dum dee dum dee dum dee dum... ready. Which one is it under Sir?

Sarge: The red one.

Zombie: Yesss, how did you know??

Sarge: Because you didn't put it under the green or blue one! One little tip Zombie - the cups have all got to be exactly the same!!

Zombie: How would I know which one it was under then!?!

Sarge: Grr! Anyway, enough of this nonsense. I've dictated a letter onto this dictaphone and need you to type it up.

Zombie: Eh?

Sarge: What? Oh... a dictaphone records my voice, you then play it and write down what is spoken. Listen. "Dear residents, in regard to your complaints about the village fete..."

Zombie: Hehehehe, how did you get into that tiny thing AND be here at the same time?? No, don't tell me, it's another magic trick!

Sarge: No not quite Zombie, but yes, I suppose I could appear to be somewhere I wasn't. Anyway, just get on with what I've asked you.

Zombie: Right you are Sarge.

Narrator: Sometime later...

Zombie: Sarge I've finished, can I practise my bit for the talent contest now?

Sarge: Your bit? You haven't got a 'bit'.

Zombie: Not yet, but if you helped me, I could.

Sarge: Oh really Zombie, OK, if I help you, will you leave me alone?

Zombie: Ooh goody goody, yes I will Sarge!

Sarge: So, first you'd introduce yourself, then maybe open with a joke.

Zombie: Like what?

Sarge: Oh...er...ah ok! "What do you call a deer with no eyes?"

Zombie: Don't know.

Sarge: No eyed deer.

Zombie: I've got no idea either...

Sarge: No Zombie. No EYED DEER.

Zombie: Oh yeah. Hehehehehe.

Sarge: Then you'd do the cup trick, then, maybe a bit of balloon modelling. Then a card trick like I showed you, then a big finale like my escape trick. Anyway, you go and practise, I'm busy.

Narrator: Zombie can be heard practising in a backroom...

Zombie: Ladies and Gentlemen, I'm the Great Zombini. I'm a great magician like Harry Potty. You will be amazed by my show which I'm going to start with a joke like what Sarge said. "What do you call a deer with no hat?" "No hat deer." Hehehehehe.

Narrator*:* Sarge happens to hear his 'show' as he passes the door…

Sarge: The Great Zombini indeed! Still… it keeps him happy.

Narrator: Zombie keeps practising every day until Saturday finally arrives

Zombie: Sarge, Sarge, Sarge, Can I do the talent show tonight? Please, please, please.

Sarge: Sorry Zombie, only one of us can do it, as someone needs to be on duty at the same time.

Zombie: Owww, please, please, please, Sarge. I really, really, really…REALLY, want to do it.

Sarge: No Zombie.

Zombie: Owww but...

Sarge: NO! Now you go and carry on practising... and maybe next year you'll be ready. He he he.

Narrator: Zombie has trundled off to his bedroom and it's now close to the time the show starts and his voice can be heard coming from behind a door in the police station...

Zombie: "This is Zombie speaking and I'm actually in this room practising my magic show - and not at the village hall. So don't come in! Especially if you are Sarge."

Sarge: Oh bless him, he's still practising. I'll give him a few more minutes, then tell him I'm off to perform, so he has to be on duty.

Narrator: Sarge waits outside the door, then hears: "This is Zombie speaking and I'm actually in this room practising my magic show - and not in the village hall..." Sarge soon realises this is a recording made on the dictaphone! When he enters, he sees the room empty, but a window wide open!

Sarge: ZOMBIE!!

Narrator: Meanwhile back at the village hall…

Zombie: Ladies and Gentlemen, I am the Great Zombini. You will be amazed by my show because I am more clever than a potato. I have been making audiences disappear for years with my magic, and I will have you rolling in the aisles with my jokes. So, without further ado, let's get started. "Why did the chicken cross the road?"

Audience: Don't know… why did the chicken cross the road??

Zombie: I don't know either, but if I see it, I will ask it, then I can tell you the answer next time I see you.

Narrator: The audience start to titter because of the stupidity of the joke. Meanwhile, Sarge can be heard off stage…

Sarge: Zombie? Zombie, where are you? I know you're here somewhere… and you're meant to be on duty!

Zombie: Ooer, I'd better hurry up…

Narrator*:* The audience start to laugh even more.

Zombie: OK, for my first trick, I will need a volunteer…

Narrator: Meanwhile, Sarge walks on stage after spotting Zombie. (He is unaware of the audience).

Sarge: Aha! There you are Zombie. You're meant to be at the station, so I can be here. You wait till I get you, you…

Zombie: Aha, Ladies and Gentlemen, my volunteer has arrived.

Narrator: The audience really start to laugh now… because they think it is all part of the act… and Sarge suddenly becomes aware of them and has to act nicely…

Audience: Hehe, haha, hoho.

Zombie: We have never met before have we Sarge? So, tell the audience your name.

Sarge: It's Terry. Terry Spicer.

Zombie: OK Mr Terrifying, I'm going to hide this ball under one of these glasses and switch them around like... this... now you have to guess which glass the ball is under...

Sarge: Under the middle glass!

Zombie: Yesss, how did you know?

Sarge: Grrr.

Zombie: Never mind, now I will make a balloon animal.

Narrator: Zombie blows and blows, but can't inflate the balloon

Zombie: Phht, phht, phht. There you have it Ladies and Gentlemen... a garden worm. And now I will do a card trick. See there is nothing up my sleeve.

Narrator: A whole deck of cards falls out all over the floor. Zombie picks up two of the cards.

Zombie: Choose a card Mr Terrible. Any card. And when you've looked at it, put it back in the pack.

Sarge: Done.

Zombie: Now I will shuffle them, and your card will be the one on top. Is THIS your card Sir?

Sarge: No.

Zombie: This one?

Sarge: Yes.

Zombie: And there you have it Ladies and Gentlemen, a successful magic trick. And now, to end my act, I will tie my assistant up, and he will escape. I'll put the handcuffs on him like this...

Sarge: Zombie, they have to be my special...

Zombie: And throw the blanket over him like this...

Sarge: Zombie, I won't be able to...

Zombie: And padlock the chains like this...

Sarge: Zombie, I can't get out!

Zombie: Then I set a timer to give me enough time to get back to the police station... I mean, for my assistant to escape! I've been the Great Zombini, you've been a great audience. Thank you very much, goodnight.

Narrator: Zombie takes a bow, then hurries out and the audience laugh and clap. Meanwhile...

Sarge: Zombie, let me out of here. Zombie, do you hear me? Zombie? ZOMBIE!!

Sarge's Birthday   S1 E4

Zombie: Here you go Sarge, the local paper you asked me to get.

Sarge: Thank you Zombie, put it on my desk and I'll read it later.

Zombie: Is there anything in it about the Talent Show?

Sarge: Well, they usually have a small write up or, after one of my shows, a slightly larger one. But of course, I didn't do one this year did I Zombie? No, because you decided to steal and in fact, RUIN my act!

Zombie: Oh Sarge, could you see if there is anything about the show? Please, please, please, please.

Sarge: Oh... very well Zombie, but if I do read it to you, do you promise to leave me alone, so I can get some work done?

Zombie: Ooh goody goody, yes Sarge, I promise!

Sarge: Very well. Now let me see... "Blah,blah,blah, however, the star act of the night must have been Sergeant Spicer..." you see Zombie, I'm well thought of in the community.

Zombie: Well done Sarge. What else does it say??

Sarge: Where was I? "The star act of the night must have been Sergeant Spicer with his Great Zombini act. This new twist (on his frankly tired old magic) saw Mr Spicer making a fool of himself whilst his assistant - the Great Zombini cleverly pretended not to know magic tricks or how to make balloon animals. Indeed, he had the audience in stitches with his jokes and had them dying to see him return - where they will finally find out **why** the chicken crossed the road." Bah! Tired old magic indeed!

Zombie: Ooh, what's that story on the front page - with the fire engine on?

Sarge: I'm not reading anymore Zombie. I'll read the headline only, and then it's back to work. "Firemen rescue local man found in handcuffs under a blanket."

Zombie: Ooh, I wonder who that could be??

Narrator: Sarge hides the paper in his drawer, and he's flustered.

Sarge: Well, we'll never know - as he declined to give his name. Anyway, we've got a busy day today, because tomorrow, I don't want to be doing much, as it is a special day.

Zombie: I know why tomorrow is a special day.

Sarge: You do??

Zombie: Yes, tomorrow is special because it's Wednesday.

Sarge: That's right Zombie. Tomorrow is special because it's Wednes... you idiot! Tomorrow is special because it's my birthday. And not even the Great Zombini is going to ruin my birthday. I refuse to let him. I want a day to remember, not forget!

Zombie: Ooh, will we have cake?

Sarge: WE Zombie? I will be having cake.

Zombie: And will we... you, be having presents?

Sarge: Yes Zombie, hopefully I will. And NO Zombie, you can't open them!

Zombie: Oww. Hey Sarge...

Sarge: What is it now Zombie?

Zombie: How are birthday cakes made?

Sarge: What?? Oh, er... I suppose a basic one would require you to mix eggs, flour, butter and sugar in a bowl, then bake in the oven for about 30 minutes. Now enough of your questions, let me get on with my work.

Narrator: A little while later...

Zombie: Happy birthday to you, happy birthday to...

Sarge: What are you doing Zombie?!

Zombie: I've made you a cake Sarge, just the way you told me earlier.

Sarge: For a start Zombie, it should really be tomorrow we have cake. And secondly Zombie...

Zombie: Yes Sarge?

Sarge: Next time, you'll need to take the eggs out of their shells and the flour out of the packet when you mix them!

Zombie: Oww.

Sarge: Listen Zombie. If you really insist on doing something for my birthday, why don't you get some ideas whilst you're out on your beat down the High Street this afternoon? The bakery has a lovely looking cake in its window...

Zombie: Right you are Sarge.

Narrator: At The end of the shift, Zombie returns with a card, wrapping paper present and he's really pleased with himself.

Zombie: Hey Sarge, guess what I got you while I was out?

Sarge: No Zombie, birthdays are meant to be a surprise and when you've got a surprise, you don't tell anyone do you? Now, I'm going to get a good night's sleep, so you turn everything off, when you finish wrapping. There is a good lad. Night night.

Narrator: Zombie eventually finishes wrapping and heads to bed. The next morning...

Zombie: Happy birthday Sarge!

Sarge: Zombie, it's five in the morning!

Zombie: I know, I was too excited to sleep. I've got you a card.

Sarge: Hmmn, Well I'm awake now, so I suppose I'll open it.

Zombie: Ooh goody goody!

Sarge: Ah, I see the shopkeeper must have seen your magic show.

Zombie: Eh?

Sarge: When they said to you: "pick a card - any card," you picked – 'congratulations on the birth of your daughter'!

Zombie: Owww…

Sarge: Never mind, let's read the inside. "Dear Swarge, Happy Chris, East, Birpday, Love Z (I put Z because I can't spell Zombie)." I'll tell you how to spell Zombie… get a pen and paper and write this down. I…

Zombie: I…

Sarge: D…

Zombie: D…

Sarge: I…

Zombie: I…

Sarge: O and T.

Zombie: O and… T. Are you sure? Just that somehow, it doesn't look right…

Sarge: Oh, it is right Zombie. I'll prove it to you. How many eyes have you got?

Zombie: Two.

Sarge: Correct. And what do we do at the end of every shift?

Zombie: We do tea. Oh yeah, that's why there's a T at the end!

Sarge: Now you're getting it Zombie, and if you sign everything from now on with that spelling – I'll know it's from YOU!

Zombie: Right you are Sarge. Can I give you your present now?

Sarge: If you must. Yes, let's get it over with.

Zombie: I wrapped it myself!

Sarge: I can see that.

Zombie: I know how much you like gardening, so I bought you a plant.

Sarge: Thank you for letting me know before I've opened it Zombie.

Zombie: That's alright Sarge.

Sarge: Of course, you know what will go well with this 'plant' don't you Zombie?

Zombie: What's that Sarge?

Sarge: A pot. And a tray for the pot to stand on. Oh, and some soil. And... maybe a plant!

Zombie: Oh yeah, I forgot all those other things, but there is a plant in there... right in the corner of the wrapping.

Sarge: You mean... these two things?

Zombie: Yes! See, I didn't ruin the surprise, because you won't know what plants I got you until you patiently water them for two years...

Sarge: You're right Zombie. I can't wait to see what plant these two lemon pips grow into! Now, a nice birthday present will be you allowing me a few more hours sleep. Do you think you can do that?!

Zombie: Right you are Sarge.

Narrator: Sarge comes downstairs a few hours later...

Sarge: Ah, that's better Zombie. What have you done since I've been asleep?

Zombie: I bought a cake from the bakery.

Sarge: What, the big one in the window?

Zombie: The big, chocolate one you said looks delicious.

Sarge: The big, chocolate one with all the chocolate truffles on it?

Zombie: Yes Sarge.

Sarge: The big, chocolate, delicious looking one, with all the truffles and chocolate cream oozing out! I could almost kiss you - for buying that Zombie. Well, put it on that plate over there, and we'll have it with a cup of tea.

Zombie: It IS on that plate over there.

Sarge: Don't be silly Zombie, this plate is empt... you ate it didn't you Zombie!

Zombie: ...Yes Sarge. Oh sorry. But I got hungry while it sat there, and you were asleep... I wanted to save you some... but it was delicious, just like you thought it would be. *You* would have liked it.

Sarge: Oh look, you did save me some...

Zombie: I did?!

Sarge: Yes look. 1,2,3,4,5 – 6 crumbs! Do you mind if I have them, or shall we have 3 each!?

Zombie: You go ahead Sarge, I'm full up.

Sarge: You didn't even surprise me by lighting the **one** candle you had on it.

Zombie: I was told never to play with matches Sarge.

Sarge: Hmmmn. Well at least Mrs. Spicer has made me a cake... And THAT has loads of candles on. And NO Zombie, you are not to eat any. You're to leave it in the cardboard box it's in. Now, make me a cup of tea, and bring it into the garden. I'm going to plant these pips.

Zombie: Right you are Sarge.

Narrator: Zombie makes a cup of tea and takes it into the garden. Sarge drinks it.

Sarge: Ah, that was a lovely cup of tea Zombie.

Zombie: Sarge, can I plant pip?

Sarge: Zombie, if you haven't got the patience to wait for me to wake up before eating the cake, you won't have the patience it takes to grow a plant. Now you go and find something to do as I've had enough of you and your 'surprises' for one day.

Zombie: Well, I do have one more surprise... I lit the candles on your other cake!

Sarge: See Zombie - no patience - just as I said. Let me guess, you pretended it was *your* birthday, and blew them all out?

Zombie: Don't be silly Sarge. I put the lid back on, so it would be a surprise for when you came back in.

Sarge: Z...Z...Zombie, let me get this right... you lit a load of candles, then you put a lid over them - which is made of cardboard, and will burn. Then you left them burning... and came out here and started chatting?!

Zombie: Oops!

Narrator: The fire alarm goes off and Sarge has to call the fire brigade. They put the fire out and the Fire Chief talks to Sarge...

Fireman: Well, that's the fire out. It's mainly smoke damage you've got, so you will be able to be up and running in a couple of days. Unfortunately for tonight, the only dry part of the station is the cells. Hope you don't mind sleeping there overnight until my men can come and clear up tomorrow?

Sarge: No that's fine officer. Thank you.

Fireman: Here, don't I know you, you look familiar...

Sarge: No, no, no I don't think so. Anyway, thanks once again. Goodbye.

Narrator: Sarge ushers the fireman away, flustered... Nighttime in the cells...

Zombie: Since it's your birthday Sarge, you can choose which bunk you want to sleep in.

Sarge: That's very kind of you Zombie. Well, this certainly has been a birthday to remember.

Zombie: Oh that's good Sarge, 'cos that's what you wanted - a birthday to remember. AND being surrounded by those you love.

Sarge: Grrr, don't push it Zombie. Have you got any of that cellotape you used for wrapping leftover?

Zombie: Yes I have Sarge. Why?

Sarge: Could you put a strip over your mouth till morning then, there's a good lad. Night Zombie.

Zombie: Night Sarge.

Zombie and the Football Fans   S1 E5

Narrator: Sarge has been looking high and low for Zombie...

Sarge: Zombie, Zombie? Where are you? Ah there you are, why are you hiding under that duvet?

Zombie: 'Cos, you said soon we will be going undercover.

Sarge: Hmmn, Undercover means not wearing a uniform.

Zombie: Ooh, do we get to wear party clothes?

Sarge: No Zombie.

Zombie: Oh, you mean we're going out like this...

Narrator: Zombie stands up naked.

Sarge: Uugh Zombie, Put some clothes on! When I said we're not wearing uniform, I meant we'll be wearing ordinary clothes. We are going to dress up as football fans.

Zombie: Ooh goody goody.

Sarge: Zombie, you know nothing about football.

Zombie: Yes I do, it's round and you kick it.

Sarge: Well, you're going to need to learn a lot more than that before we do our undercover operation, or they'll guess that you're not really a football supporter. What clubs have you heard of?

Zombie: Oh, that's easy. A golf club, a nightclub, the ace of clubs...

Sarge: I mean FOOTBALL clubs you idiot!

Zombie: Oww. Erm...Tottenham...

Sarge: Good. Do you know their full name?

Zombie: Yes. Tottenham Forest!

Sarge: Idiot!

Zombie: Then there's Liverpool United. And Manchester.

Sarge: United or City?

Zombie: Yep – 'Manchester United Or City'.

Sarge: No Zombie, I mean there are two main teams in Manchester. United and City. And it's plain old Liverpool - by the way.

Zombie: I support Liverpool-by-the-way.

Sarge: Oh God! OK Zombie let's try something else. West Ham are called the Hammers. So, what picture do you think they have on their badge?

Zombie: A car?

Sarge: No, I'll give you a clue. It's something to do with tools...

Zombie: Oh yeah, a screwdriver!

Sarge: No, come on, think...

Zombie: A saw? A wrench, a spanner?

Sarge: No. Stop. I'll tell you. One of their nicknames is the Hammers so they have a hammer on their badge. Let's try another. Wolverhampton Wanderers are nicknamed Wolves, what do they have on their badge?

Zombie: Oh yeah, I get it... a wolf?

Sarge: Very good Zombie. And what do you think Arsenal have on their badge?

Zombie: That's easy it must be an...

Sarge: Ah, Chief Inspector, I was just briefing Zombie on our undercover operation to infiltrate the football gang.

Chief Inspector: Good, good. That's what I have just popped in to talk to you about. Our intelligence says they will be meeting at the pub today and, as it is Quiz Night, you could pretend to be a quiz team and sit near their table so you could overhear their conversation.

Zombie: Ooh goody goody, a quiz.

Chief Inspector: Ah, that's what I like to see, an enthusiastic officer. You must be really proud of him Spicer?

Sarge: Hmmmn…

Narrator: **Sarge carries on trying to educate Zombie ready for their undercover operation for the Quiz Night before they head off…**

Sarge: Right, this is the place - The King's Arms. Now, these people are very dangerous, so no doing anything silly, or you might cause a riot.

Zombie: Right you are Sarge.

Sarge: Oh, and one more thing Zombie, no drinking alcohol.

Zombie: Right you are Sarge… what's alcohol?

Sarge: Never mind, just get inside and find a table whilst I find out where the football hooligans are sitting.

Narrator: Zombie finds a table and Sarge finds the table the thugs are sitting around and starts listening in to their conversation...

City fan 1: We don't want Doug on our team, he's useless and an idiot, he'd ruin our chances of winning the quiz. Go speak to that stupid looking bloke and see if you can join his team.

Doug: What, the one with the moustache standing near us?

City fan 2: No, the one sitting on that table over there.

Narrator: The hooligans point to Zombie's table and Doug goes over.

Doug: 'Ere mate, can I join you? My mates don't want me to sit on their team, they think I'm an idiot.

Zombie: My mate Sarge thinks I'm an idiot too. So, we can be on the same team. What shall we call ourselves?

Doug: The 3 Idiots?

Zombie: Yeah!

Landlord: OK Ladies and Gentlemen, most of you will know the rules, but just to recap: No cheating by using mobile phones. No hanging around other tables to listen to that team's answers. And as usual, halfway through; the team whose name we pick out of the raffle - wins the half bottle of Fire Water vodka. Good luck.

Doug: 'Ere mate, can you look after my mobile so that the Landlord knows I'm not cheating?

Zombie: Sure.

Landlord: OK, an easy question to start - what's the meaning of the word 'cancel'?

Doug: Hur, Hur, that's easy...they're the people who mend the roads and empty the bins in London!

Zombie: Oww, write that down.

Landlord: OK question two. What is a semi-conductor?

Zombie: Is it someone who works part time with an orchestra?

Doug: I suppose it must be; I'll write it down.

Landlord: Question 3. Geography. Along from Brighton on the south coast is a place called Saltdean. What is the next town along called?

Doug & Zombie: It must be... Pepperdean!

Narrator: The quiz continues, and Sarge continues to try to listen in on the hooligan's conversation, but the hooligans notice him...

City fan 1: 'Ere, that idiot with the moustache, seems to be listening to our answers and writing things down. You don't think he's part of United's Quiz Team, do you?!

City fan 2: Dunno, wait to see if he's doing it during the second half of the quiz, then we'll 'ave a word with 'im - if he is! Anyway, quiet now, I wanna see who's won the vodka...

Landlord: And... the winner of the Fire Water is... The 3 Idiots.

Doug: Ooh goody goody.

Zombie: Yeah, and lucky it's only water, 'cos my mate Sarge said I'm not allowed to drink alcohol. I'll have a big glass thanks Doug.

Doug: Right you are Zombie, and I will too. Cheers!

Narrator: Zombie and Doug soon become drunk and slide under the table giggling and being stupid…

Zombie: Question 15. Why don't pirates take a bath before walking the plank? Hic!

Doug: 'Cos they'll wash ashore later. Hic!

Doug & Zombie: He he he he he. Hic!

Doug: Why did the gangster stand in concrete?

Zombie: Because he wanted to be a hardened criminal!

Doug & Zombie: He he he he he he. Hic!

Narrator: Meanwhile, Sarge is seen hanging around both United's and the City quiz tables and both teams have noticed…

United fan 1: Oi, City, stop sending you mate over to listen to our answers!

City fan 2: 'E aint our mate, you keep sending him over here to listen to our answers! You cheaters!

United fan 2: If anyone's a cheater it's your lot. You had to dive to get a last-minute penalty, last week!

City fan 1: You calling us cheaters!?

United fan 1: Yeah, what of it??!

City fan 2: You wanna come here and say that?

United fan 2: Yeah, come on then...

Narrator: Tables go flying and a riot starts. Sarge gets caught up in the mess, but Zombie and Doug are still drunk under the table. Eventually the emergency services come and restore order.

Policeman: Any idea who started it pal?

Ambulance driver: Witnesses are saying it's that bloke with the moustache in the ambulance over there getting his head bandaged.

Policeman: Right, I'll be having a word with him then.

Ambulance driver: I'm afraid it may be a while before he's fit to interview. He's taken quite a knock to his head and keeps insisting he's a Sergeant in the police force and to ask a zombie if we don't believe him!

Policeman: You don't think he's a bit... you know...

Ambulance driver: Wacko? Possibly. I think we'll keep him in for a few days to run some tests.

Policeman: And what about these two?

Narrator: The policeman points to Zombie and Doug.

Ambulance driver: Just a couple of drunks as far as I can tell. Haven't got any cuts or bruises, so not involved with the brawl.

Doug: Oi, officer, what did the policeman say to his tummy?

Policeman: What??

Doug: You're under a vest. Hur, hur. Hic!

Policeman: You'll be under a vest, I mean - under arrest, in a minute if you carry on. Besides, don't I know you?

Doug: Er... no.

Policeman: Yes I do, you're 'Doug the Thug' – football hooligan and phone thief.

Doug: Well, I haven't got a phone on me.

Policeman: I don't believe you!

Zombie: It's true, he gave it to me earlier to look after. Here.

Policeman: Thank you very much. I'll take that for evidence, it will have all your hooligan contacts in.

Doug: Hur, Hur. Unlucky copper, that's not my phone.

Policeman: I bet it is!

Doug: No it's not, that's the one I stole from someone in the pub earlier... oops!

Policeman: Aha, you're nicked! And if *you* don't want to find yourself nicked too, I suggest you find your way home - right away.

Zombie: Right you are oshifer... See you later Doug.

Doug: See you later Zombie.

Narrator*:* **The police car pulls off and as Zombie staggers away... all that could be heard from the car is...**

Doug: "I know a song that will really get on your nerves...really get on your nerves...really..."

Zombie and Zombier   S1E6

Chief Inspector: Bad news I'm afraid Zombie. Sarge has taken a bang to the head so won't be in today, and as PC Smith has COVID, you will be in charge.

Zombie: Ooh goody goody!

Chief Inspector: The good news is you won't be doing it on your own, a new recruit will be here in under an hour.

Zombie: Ooh baddy baddy!

Chief Inspector: Right, well I'll leave you to get ready Zombie, but don't be phoning Sarge every 5 minutes, the man has been told to get some rest. Use your initiative if you have a problem. Good day.

Narrator: **Chief Inspector leaves and Zombie role-plays being in charge…**

Zombie: Right new recruit, let's get one thing clear, I'm in charge and I run a 'tight ship' around here. Is that understood?

'New recruit':   Right you are Sir.

Zombie: And new recruit, why have you got a fishing rod??

'New recruit': Because you said you run a tight ship...

Zombie: No, no, no, no. When we say a 'tight ship', we mean we like things orderly. Dear oh dear, I can see you're going to need a lot of training.

Zombie 2: Excuse me...

Zombie: Hold on will you, I'm just talking to my new recruit.

Zombie 2: Really? Well, I didn't see anyone...

Zombie: Yeah well... he...erm... he popped out to the shops. How can I help you?

Zombie 2: Chief Inspector sent me. I'm the new recruit. But if you've already got a new recruit, I'll go back and tell him.

Zombie: No, no, no, no...er... no need to tell Chief Inspector... I'll fire the first new recruit... when he gets back from the shops. Anyway welcome, my name is Zombie.

Zombie 2: It can't be - MY name is Zombie.

Zombie: How will we tell each other apart in that case??

Zombie 2: Dunno... is there someone here who can tell us what to do?

Zombie: There is one person who tells me what to do, but I've been told not to ring them.

Zombie 2: We can ask that new recruit when he gets back...

Zombie: Nah, I've just remembered, I can ring him... once.

Sarge: Hello? Who's this? Zombie... aha... you're in charge!! Dear Lord no! What? New recruit... Oh good. It's another zombie! Dear Lord no! Two of you. I don't know whether to laugh or cry...

Zombie: And so, I was wondering Sarge, if they're a zombie and I'm a zombie and there called Zombie and I'm called Zombie, how will we tell each other apart?

Sarge: Well, who's the tallest?

Zombie: I am.

Sarge: Well, there you go then.

Zombie: Ah, but what if they stood on a chair?

Sarge: Precisely - what if they stood on a chair? WHAT IF THEY STOOD ON A CHAIR! Idiot! No no, I must keep calm to help my recovery. OK Zombie, you've got dark hair, what colour is theirs?

Zombie: Blonde.

Sarge: Well, there you go, no wait, let me guess - what if they dyed it?

Zombie: Exactly.

Sarge: Look, you be Zombie 1, and they can be Zombie 2.

Zombie: That's a good idea Sarge, I'll tell her that...

Sarge: Her? Her! ZOMBIE!

Zombie: Right, Sarge said I'm Zombie 1 and you're Zombie 2.

Zombie 2:   Right you are Zombie 1.

Zombie: OK, let's show you how to make a cup of tea... you'll mainly be in charge of that... and we drink a lot of tea here you'll find. Now, this is called a kettle, and once we've filled it up with water, we press *this* button to boil the water. Then pour it on top of a bag. Which we put into these things - called cups. Then we add milk and sugar. Do you think you could do that whilst I check to see if there are any messages?

Zombie 2:   Right you are Zombie 1.

Narrator: Zombie obviously has no idea how to check for phone messages so phones Sarge to ask...

Sarge: Ah Zombie, lovely to hear from you again. It's only been... 4 minutes since you last rang!

Zombie: Oh that's good, 'cos Chief Inspector told me not to ring you every 5 minutes.

Sarge: Hmmmn. Let me guess... you want to know how to get the lid off the coffee? Or, because they're both brushes, can you use a loo brush to clean your teeth? Or maybe, are traffic cones just big ice-cream cones?

Zombie: Yeah. But also, how do I retrieve any messages?

Sarge: Don't you worry about that. But if you hear anything important on the police radio, you are to let Upper Ringclay deal with it, you hear? And you are to send Zombie 2 out to anything easy to deal with. And you're to stay there clear?

Zombie: Right you are Sarge.

Zombie 2: I've made you a cup of tea Zombie.

Zombie: Why is there a plastic bag in my cup?

Zombie 2: You said pour the hot water on top of the bag.

Zombie: Ooer, what would Sarge do in this situation? Oh yeah, I've got it. ZOMBIE!

Zombie 2: Why are you shouting at yourself Zombie?

Zombie: I'm not, I'm being Saaarge and I'm shouting at yooou.

Zombie 2: No, I'm Zombie 2, remember?!

Zombie: Oh yeah. Alright, go back out and try again.

Zombie 2: Oh OK. I'll just go out...and re-enter...hold on... I've made you a cup of tea Zombie.

Zombie: ZOMBIE...2. When we say bags, we mean TEA bags! Never mind, I did the same when I was your age and I started policemanning. Right, you man the police scanner radio, like what PC Smith would do, and I'll walk up and down and scowl a lot, like what Sarge would do...

Zombie 2: Right you are Zombie 1.

Zombie: And you can be in charge of dusting and cleaning, 'cos this equipment could do with a good dust.

Zombie 2: Right you are.

Narrator: Just then the police radio crackles into life... "Report of a serious crime in progress at the old Vicarage, over."

Zombie: Ooh, the police will have to dust for fingerprints.

Zombie 2: We ARE the police…aren't we?

Zombie: Oh yeah, that's right, we are!

Zombie 2: And you said I'm in charge of dusting, so shall I head down there? Or are you not allowed to make that kind of decision?

Zombie: No, I am allowed to make decisions. Chief Inspector told me to use my initials. So, take all the cleaning equipment and get down to the old Vicarage - quickly.

Zombie 2: Right you are Zombie 1.

Zombie: Aah, Sarge's face will be a picture when he finds out…

Narrator: Zombie 2 returns after quite a while…

Zombie: You've been gone a long time.

Zombie 2: Yeah, the place was the right mess. There were broken things everywhere, footprints and fingerprints everywhere, blood all over the place. I tell you; it took me ages to get it clean enough to take my Instagram photos.

Zombie: Ooh, ooh, let me see... Who's that bloke with the knife standing over that body?

Zombie 2: Don't know. Told him to get out because he was photobombing my pictures, and to take his mate with him. So, the last few photos show the place fully cleaned. Like nobody had ever been there. The owners will be pleased.

Zombie: Yeah, and so will Sarge. I can imagine his face... right now...

Right, let's celebrate. Read out how much money is in the petty-cash book.

Zombie 2: Minus £1 for glass broken by Zombie when his shoelace came undone. Minus £3 for Zombie wasting breakfast cereal. Minus £5000 for the fire brigade being called out when Zombie burnt down the police station...

Zombie: Yes, yes, but there must be some money going in...?

Zombie 2: Oh yes...here. Plus 5p Zombie found down the back of the sofa.

Zombie: Well there you go, so what's the grand total??

Zombie 2: Minus £7390.40p.

Zombie: Give...that...to me!

Narrator: Zombie takes the petty-cash book and changes the minus sign into a plus sign.

Zombie: Right, now we've got plus £7390.40p to spend.

Zombie 2: Ooh goody goody.

Zombie: Right quiet, I'm making a phone call. Hello, is that the Rainforest Delivery company? Good. I'd like to order a PlayStation and games. 2 controllers and two gaming chairs. Some popcorn, sweets, sausage rolls, crips, cakes and fizzy drinks. A bubble gum machine, jukebox, and a pinball machine. And I'll pay the £200 extra to have it delivered right away. Thanks. Bye.

Narrator: Soon, both zombies are busy gaming and snacking once their delivery comes.

Zombie: Broom, brooom, broooom. Scoff, scoff, munch, munch.

Zombie 2: Ack, ack, ack, take THAT 'baddies', chomp, chomp, crunch, crunch.

Zombie: Pass us another packet of popcorn Zombie 2, I'm gonna need to fill up on snacks to complete this mission.

Narrator: Whilst they've been busy gaming, Sarge has turned up at the front desk - still in bandages after discharging himself from hospital.

Zombie 2: Right you are Zombie 1. And what shall I tell this bloke who is at the front desk covered in bandages and is asking to speak to you?

Zombie: Tell him to go away and come back another day. Tell him: "I'm doing police training what is very important."

Narrator: At this point, Sarge is standing behind the 2 zombies, but they don't really notice because they are engrossed in gaming...

Sarge: Oh yes Zombie, I can see you're doing 'police training'. If you go left at this house and look in the red cupboard, you'll find a power-up.

Zombie: Yes, yes. I already know that. Don't tell me what to do, you sound just like my old boss.

Sarge: Your old boss??

Zombie: Yes yes, he sounded just like you, but wore a policeman's helmet instead of having bandages on his head. Moan, moan, moan is all he did. They had to get rid of him in the end and replace him with me. Mind you, you have got a silly moustache like his one.

Sarge: I see, so, if I kept this silly moustache, took my bandages off like... this... and put this police helmet on... who would I look like now??!

Narrator: Zombie suddenly realises!

Zombie: Why, you'd look like...Sahahaarge. How nice to see you back. Zombie 2, WHAT IS ALL THIS STUFF DOING HERE? I thought I told you to get rid of it. You're fired!

Sarge: And is there an explanation for all this 'stuff' being here?

Zombie: Well, you know when you've cleaned up a case - that you celebrate?

Sarge: Yes, with a box of chocolates or small bottle of wine, not a gaming and snack emporium!! Please don't tell me you've tackled a SERIOUS crime...?!

Zombie: Not just tackled, cleaned up the whole crime...

Narrator: Zombie proceeds to tell Sarge everything...Sarge laughs nervously, worried...

Sarge: Ha, ha, ha. So, let me get this straight. You took charge and sent Zombie 2 out to a serious crime scene. They thought 'cleaning up' a crime scene meant, cleaning all the fingerprints, footprints, blood, broken things – the things that we call 'evidence', so there's no trace of any crime. Then Zombie 2 saw the perpetrator standing over the body with a knife and told them to get out and take the body with them!? I've only got one thing to say to you...ZOMBIE!!!

The Award Ceremony   S1E7

Zombie: Sarge, why are you dressed as a waiter?

Sarge: I'm not dressed as a waiter Zombie; I'm trying on my outfit for the upcoming Local Area Award ceremony. They do have waiters there, because it is at a big posh hotel, but they're only there to serve drinks to those guests who are wining and dining.

Zombie: Why would you whine if you're being served a lovely meal?

Sarge: Not that kind of whine you idiot. Wine the drink.

Zombie: Owww. So, what's the Local Area Award Ceremony?

Sarge: It's where local businesses and services get recognised for what they have contributed to the community. Best small business, best small bus service, best police station etc...

Zombie: What's the local area?

Sarge: Zombie, are you really that stupid? Every day, you walk past THIS map of the local area, have you never thought to look at it?

Zombie: Er...no.

Sarge: Right! I'm going to teach you about Ringclay - our local area, particularly since my family have been here for generations. This whole area is Ringclay - so named because the whole area is surrounded by a ring of clay.

Zombie: Owww...

Sarge: This area is Upper Ringclay, and people have been living there since Roman times. In fact, they say you can recognise a resident from Upper Ringclay just by their face - the 'Upper Ringclay face' - they call it.

Zombie: Owww...

Sarge: And our area we are in charge of is Ringclay Bottom.

Zombie: So, when the local see you, do they think of you as someone with a wrinkly bottom face?

Sarge: Yes, they probably do Zombie. They probably say: "he's got a Ringclay Bottom face".

Zombie: He he he he.

Sarge: Oh honestly Zombie, you can be so childish at times. I'm glad you won't be coming with me to the ceremony.

Zombie: Ooh goody goody!

Sarge: Well, that's a surprise reaction. I thought you'd be all: "Oh, please, please, please".

Zombie: I do want to go, but if I don't, I'll be in charge here. I'll go and practise.

Sarge: Yes, Zombie you go and practise being in charge.

Narrator: Sarge then realises what he has said…

Sarge: Oh God no! I'd better ring Chief Inspector.

Narrator: A while later, Zombie can be heard having a conversation with himself - role-playing being in charge…

Zombie: "Zombie, I'm off to the ceremony, you're in charge of PC Broom while I'm away."

"Right you are Sarge." "OK PC Broom let's get one thing straight, I'm in charge here."

"Right you are Sergeant Zombie, since you are the cleverest person invented." "What should I do?"

"You could start by cleaning this mess up - since you're a broom."

"Right you are Sergeant Zombie."

Sarge: Zombie, have you seen the broom, I've got something I need to sweep up?

Narrator: Zombie opens the door slightly and hands Sarge the broom by only thrusting his arm through the gap.

Zombie: Er, there you go Sarge. No need to come in.

Sarge: What are you up to Zombie?

Zombie: Nothing Sarge.

Narrator: Sarge goes off to sweep, but is soon back...

Sarge: Zombie, I can't sweep the floor properly because someone has cut out some of the bristles. I know it would have been you. And why are you hiding your face behind that tea towel? Give... it... here.

Zombie: Ooer...

Sarge: Why on earth have you cut the bristles from the broom and stuck them on your face as a moustache?!

Zombie: I was practising being *you*, for when I'm put in charge.

Sarge: You're not going to be put in charge Zombie. I've just spoken to Chief Inspector, and he's getting PC Smith to cover for us. Unfortunately, that means I've got to take you with me. So, while I'm out buying a new broom and getting your outfit, you can tidy up... and get rid of that silly looking moustache.

Zombie: Right you are Sarge.

Narrator: Sarge returns a while later. Zombie has cleared up but is still wearing the moustache.

Sarge: I thought I told you to remove that moustache?

Zombie: I tried to Sarge, but it won't come off!

Sarge: Let me guess, you stuck it on with super glue, didn't you?

Zombie: Er... yes Sarge.

Sarge: You're an idiot! Well, that will teach you. You'll have to walk around looking ridiculous until the glue wears off.

Narrator: The day of the ceremony arrives, and Zombie has still got the moustache.

Zombie: I've still can't get the moustache off Sarge. What should I do??

Sarge: You'll have to be patient Zombie for a few more days at least I'm afraid. Hopefully we'll get a small table at the back where we can hide quietly. I don't want you showing me up in front of the mayor, business leaders or Chief Inspector.

Narrator: Zombie goes off and returns in his outfit…

Zombie: How do I look?

Sarge: Well, you look like a Spanish waiter, but at least you look presentable. Anyway, I'm going to practise my acceptance speech - just in case we win 'best police station award'.

Zombie: Ooh goody goody. Sarge, if we win the award, can I...

Sarge: No Zombie, I'll go up to collect it.

Zombie: Owww...

Narrator: Sarge starts his speech and Zombie listens intently...

Sarge: Ladies and Gentlemen, may I just say on behalf of the Ringclay Bottom community, how proud I am to receive this award. Of course, in receiving this I must thank a lot of people. Without whom, winning this would not be possible. First of all, I'd like to thank...

Zombie: Zombie!

Sarge: And *that's* why I didn't want you coming Zombie. If you call out during the speeches, they will call security and throw you out - no matter who you are. It's very posh there and the guests can be very snobby. But they are very influential. So, you'll end up out in the cold whilst the ceremony is on if you misbehave. Do you understand?

Zombie: Yes Sarge.

Narrator: They manage to get there without incident, but their table is right at the front.

Sarge: Oh blast, our two-person table is right at the front.

Zombie: Maybe that's because we are going to win an award?

Sarge: Ooh, maybe Zombie. You better not show me up in that case.

Zombie: I won't I promise. But I think I'll go to the loo 'cos I'm feeling nervous.

Sarge: Hehe, yes you do that Zombie. I'm used to this kind of occasion, so don't need to.

Narrator: On his way to the loo, a posh lady mistakes Zombie for a waiter…

Posh lady: Waiter, fetch me a bottle of wine please.

Zombie: Sorry lady, I'm on my way to the loo.

Posh man: My wife has just asked you for a bottle of wine, now snap to it.

Zombie: But I'm not a waiter, my name is Zombie.

Posh lady: You're right you're not a waiter the way you're behaving, and we're not interested in your name. Now, are you going to get our wine, or do you want me to speak to your boss?

Zombie: No, no, no, don't do that... here you go, there's a bottle of wine.

Narrator: Zombie reaches over and takes a bottle of wine off the table next to the lady and her husband before dashing to the loo.

Manager: I trust everything is to your liking and you are ready to order now?

Posh man: Yes, we are ready to order. We thought we'd start with the soup, then have the steak and finish with the trifle.

Manager: Very good Sir. And each table will have their own dedicated waiter. Have you met yours?

Posh lady: Yes, that's him there, heading to the front where the awards tables are. Go and get him back.

Manager: I will Madam.

Narrator: Zombie is intercepted by the Manager and given two bowls of soup to serve to the posh table.

Zombie: That man said to give you these.

Posh man: About time waiter. Now get some more wine for us.

Zombie: Yes SIR!

Posh lady: And less of the attitude man.

Zombie: Yes Sir! I mean yes Ma'am! Here's your wine. Anything else before I sit down?

Posh man: Yes, get our steaks. We've finish with this soup.

Zombie: Blimey, you ate those quickly!

Posh lady: How dare you be rude. Bring your manager back with our steaks and bring more wine.

Zombie: Here's your steaks.

Posh man: They're half eaten!

Zombie: Well, I couldn't eat a whole one! But I did bring you your wine.

Posh lady: Husband, call the Manager.

Manager: Is everything alright Sir?

Posh man: No! This man has taken wine off another table, been rude to us, served us half our food...

Manager: I'm sorry Sir, there will be no charge for the food, and I will send him off to get your trifle. Off you go... and do your shoelace up while you're at it.

Zombie: Yes Sir! But she keeps whining, and he keeps dining.

Manager: I'm sorry about that Sir, Madam. If he causes you any further distress, I'll have him removed.

Narrator: Zombie comes with the trifles, trips over his laces and gets the trifle all over the couple. They call for security and Zombie hides under a table.

Security: What is it Madam, Sir?

Posh lady: That stupid man with a moustache, has ruined our clothes and day, we want him thrown out! Before we *leave*!

Security: Sir, what does he look like?

Posh man: Stupid looking with a great big moustache. There! That looks like him on that little table down the front!

Narrator: The security guard heads to the table that they have pointed at...

Security: Excuse me Sir, we'd like you to leave...

Sarge: W... w...what?!?

Security: Don't argue Sir, you'll make a scene in front of all these people.

Sarge: B...b...but...

Security: Now Sir! Off you go. And don't come back!

Narrator: Sarge is escorted by the security guard out of the hotel where it is starting to rain. Sarge can only watch the Awards through the window...

Sarge: Grrr, I bet it's that Zombie's fault!

Narrator: Back inside, the compere is announcing the 'best police station' award and the winner is Ringclay Bottom. Zombie realises Sarge isn't there to collect the award, so goes up to collect the award, loving the opportunity to get it himself.

Zombie: Thank you Ladies and Gentlemen. I am the real Sarge. Look, I've even got his moustache. I'm not Zombie dressed up... honest. Talking of Zombie, I would like to thank him very much. He is the cleverest person I know, and I couldn't do it without him. So, if Chief Inspector is here, I ask you to put Zombie in charge of the police station from now on. Thank you and goodnight.

Sarge: Zombie, you... wait... until... I... get... hold... of...YOU!

Zombie and the Kittens   S1E8

Narrator: Sarge turns up to the police station with a cardboard box.

Zombie: Ooh Sarge, Sarge, what's in the box you're carrying?

Sarge: Never you mind Zombie, I'm looking after it for my daughter for a few days.

Zombie: Isn't your daughter old enough to look after her own cardboard box?

Sarge: You really are an idiot Zombie aren't you! It's not the box she wants me to look after, it's what's inside.

Zombie: Ooh, ooh, what's inside? And what's making that 'meowing' sound?

Sarge: Oh come on Zombie, what animal says 'meow'?

Zombie: Er...a dog?

Sarge: No.

Zombie: A mouse?

Sarge: Noo!

Zombie: An elephant?

Sarge: Oh come on Zombie, look at the size of the box, what would fit into a box this size?

Zombie: Oh yes of course... a microwave!

Sarge: Grrr. No, you fool, it's my daughter's cat. She's called Tiddles.

Zombie: That's a strange name to call your daughter!

Sarge: It's not my daughter's name, Tiddles is the cat!

Zombie: Ooh... can I see Tiddly, please, please, please.

Sarge: TIDDLES! Oh OK.

Zombie: Owww, how cute. I can see why she's not called Tiddly now - she's quite fat isn't she?

Sarge: Zombie, you know it is a bit rude to say something is 'fat', but yes, I'm a bit concerned about her weight, so think I'll take her to the vet. I'll just give them a ring. And Zombie, don't touch the cat whilst I'm on the phone, there's a good chap.

Zombie: Right you are Sarge.

Narrator: Sarge rings the vet and after the call, find Zombie looking sheepish.

Sarge: You tried to stroke her, didn't you?

Zombie: No!

Sarge: Then why have you got a cat scratch on your hand?

Zombie: Alright, I did try to stroke it, but it got cross with me. Can't we give her back to your daughter now?

Sarge: No we can't Zombie, my daughter is expecting a baby, so can't look after Tiddles at the moment.

Zombie: Can't her husband wait in for the postman?

Sarge: Why would he wait indoors when he's got to go to the hospital?

Zombie: Oh, I didn't know he was ill...

Sarge: He's not ill, he's taking my daughter to the hospital.

Zombie: Oh, it's your daughter who is ill?

Sarge: No, my daughter is expecting a baby.

Zombie: So why doesn't she wait in for the postman??

Sarge: Oh God Zombie, you really haven't got a clue, have you? When we say someone is expecting a baby, we mean they are pregnant. The woman grows the baby inside her tummy until it's ready to be born, then they go to the hospital where the doctors help her to have the baby.

Zombie: Oh, I see now. Why didn't you say that in the first place!

Sarge: Grrr. Anyway, enough of your nonsense, I need you to take the cat to the vets as I've got to stay here just in case my daughter phones. At least I can trust you not to open the box again, now she scratched you.

Zombie: Yeah, stupid Tiddlywinks.

Sarge: Tiddles! Anyway, you catch the bus at that stop over the road.

Zombie: What, the one where the fa...large lady is standing?

Sarge: Yes... don't say anything to her about her size, do you hear me?

Zombie: Right you are Sarge.

Narrator: Zombie goes over the road and Sarge watches...

Zombie: 'Scuse me lady, but when's it due?

Lady: How dare you suggest I'm pregnant, I'm normally this size.

Narrator: The lady hits Zombie with her handbag and Sarge hits his face with his palm and groans.

Zombie: I meant, when is the bus due? Silly old…

Narrator: The bus comes, Zombie goes to the vet and returns a while later excited.

Zombie: Sarge, Sarge, Sarge. Guess what? Tiddles isn't overweight, she's pregnant! The vet said.

Sarge: Oh my. Well, don't open the lid because Tiddles will run off to find somewhere to have her babies.

Zombie: Oops… too late.

Sarge: You idiot! Right, make sure all the doors are shut, so Tiddles remains in the police station. She'll find somewhere comfortable to give birth.

Zombie: Right you are Sarge.

Sarge: You'd better find Tiddles Zombie, or my daughter will 'have kittens'!

Zombie: Is your daughter a cat too then?

Sarge: Don't be daft Zombie, it's a saying. 'Having kittens' means becoming nervous or upset by something.

Zombie: Oh, she will be upset. I'm sorry.

Sarge: Don't worry, we'll find her.

Narrator: Zombie and Sarge search until bedtime - without luck.

Zombie: I'm worried now, we still haven't found her.

Sarge: Don't worry, just get into bed and we'll look in the morning.

Zombie: I can't, there is something wriggly in there. Let me hit it with a stick.

Sarge: No, no, no, no Zombie. Wait. It might be Tiddles. Have a look.

Zombie: Nah it's not a cat, but there are three little Tiddles. Hahahaha. Is this one of your magic tricks?

Sarge: Those are her kittens! She must have given birth.

Zombie: Ooh goody, goody. Can I have one?

Sarge: No Zombie, you can't! They need their mother.

Zombie: Why?

Sarge: Because she's the one who feeds them.

Zombie: I'll go and get some crisps then.

Sarge: No Zombie, she feeds the milk.

Zombie: I'll go and get...

Sarge: No Zombie, not *that* kind of milk. When a mummy has a baby, she can use milk from her body to help her baby grow. The babies rely on their mum a lot, until they can start doing things for themselves.

Zombie: Then can I look after them?

Sarge: We'll see. I'll look after them first though. You make a comfortable bed in that box, and I'll keep it under my desk for now.

Zombie: Right you are Sarge.

Narrator: A couple of days pass, but Sarge hasn't had news yet.

Sarge: Zombie, you've cleaned my desk area three times this morning, can't you find somewhere else to clean?

Zombie: Owww...

Sarge: You're trying to see the kittens, aren't you?

Zombie: No...yes. Ow Please, please, please can I hold one?

Sarge: No Zombie. Go and find something else to do.

Zombie: I know, I'll cook you breakfast...and bring it to your desk.

Sarge: Oh, a second breakfast... lovely.

Zombie: There you go Sarge.

Sarge: Lovely, but next time, can you cook the eggs... and the bacon... and the toast!?

Zombie: Owww...

Sarge: And why has the smoke alarm gone off - if you haven't been cooking? Are you trying to get my attention??

Zombie: Yesss, because you have been paying attention to the kittens all this time.

Sarge: I'm sorry Zombie, but babies need a lot of love, care and attention.

Zombie: I could do that.

Sarge: Oh no, no, no, no Zombie. God knows what would happen if I gave you a kitten. Anyway, quiet for a moment, that's my daughter ringing, we might have to head to the hospital.

Narrator: Sarge has a brief conversation; then gets his coat and car keys.

Zombie: Was that your daughter?

Sarge: Yes, so get your coat Zombie, we're going to the hospital.

Zombie: I could stay here...and look after the kit...

Sarge: No Zombie, unfortunately, I'd prefer you came with me - where I can keep an eye on you.

Zombie: Owww... I could stay here and be in charge of the poli...

Sarge: Definitely not! PC Smith is coming on duty to man the police station. And here he is now. Right Zombie, get in the car. And when we get there, you're to be on your best behaviour. No being silly, no wandering off, no making a nuisance of yourself. You hear Zombie?

Zombie: Right you are Sarge.

Narrator: They arrived at the hospital and speak to staff.

Sarge: We're here to see my daughter. She's having a baby.

Nurse: Yes, she's with the doctor now, so if you wait in this waiting room, we'll come and get you when she's ready.

Sarge: Right you are nurse. Zombie, sit with me.

Zombie: Right you are Sarge. Sarge, how long have we been here waiting?

Sarge: 3 minutes Zombie, why?

Zombie: I'm bored.

Sarge: See Zombie - no patience. We may be hours waiting here, so you'd better find some way to occupy yourself. Here, here's some money. Go and get us a nice cup of tea from that vending machine we passed on the way here.

Zombie: Right you are Sarge.

Narrator: Zombie gets distracted on the way and entertains himself by smiling and waving at the patients in another ward then ducking down and popping up behind the glass ward door...

Patient one: Nurse, nurse, there's a zombie outside.

Nurse: Nonsense, there's no such things as zombies.

Patient two: Nurse, nurse, they are right, there is a zombie!

Nurse: You two are kidders, there's nobody at the door.

Patient three: There is, we just saw him!

Nurse: Alright, I'll open the door to show you.

Narrator: Zombie hears her coming - so runs off. The nurse opens the door to no one...

Nurse: See patients - no zombie!

Narrator: Meanwhile, Sarge has gone in search of Zombie, because his daughter has given birth.

Sarge: Where have you been Zombie? I've been looking all over for you. They are ready to see us now...

Zombie: Ooh, goody goody.

Narrator: Sarge kisses his daughter and congratulates his son-in-law and introduces Zombie.

Sarge: May I hold him?

Daughter: Yes of course.

Narrator: Sarge holds his grandson, and a tear of joy runs down his cheek.

Zombie: Sarge, you're crying.

Sarge: Er yes, a bit of dust must have got in my eye.

Zombie: He really looks like you.

Sarge: Do you think so Zombie?

Zombie: Yes, because he's bald, toothless and crying.

Narrator: Everyone gives a wry smile. Sarge doesn't see the joke but carries on cuddling his grandson. Photos are taken and eventually Sarge and Zombie then head back...

Zombie: Was it nice to hold your grandson Sarge?

Sarge: Yes, yes it was Zombie. And I know you didn't get to hold him, but I tell you what...

Zombie: What Sarge?

Sarge: When we get back, you can hold the kittens.

Zombie: Ooh, goody goody... thank you Sarge. I'll be really gentle like what you were when you held your tiny grandson.

Narrator: Both drive back with a big smile on their faces...

Zombie and the Holiday   S1E9

Narrator: Sarge is just finishing up on a phone call…

Sarge: … well that's sorted then, you need a break and I need a break, so meet me here in your camper van on Friday and we'll have a nice relaxing, long weekend… just the two of us. Love you darling, bye.

Zombie: Ooh, ooh, who was that Sarge?

Sarge: Never you mind Zombie! And anyway, you shouldn't listen in on other people's conversations, it's rude.

Zombie: I didn't.

Sarge: Good. But I'm still not going to tell you who it was.

Zombie: It was your daughter, and you're planning on going to Wales this weekend. And the place you're going to has a hot tub and a sauna. And you are going to go to…

Sarge: So, you **did** listen in on my phone conversation!

Zombie: No… yes. Oh Sarge, will you please, please, please…

Sarge: No!

Zombie: Oww, but I promise I'll...

Sarge: No! You'll rabbit on and on all the way there. You'll make a nuisance of yourself in front of my daughter whilst there. You'll do daft and annoying things all weekend, and I'll need another holiday to get over this one! Nope, it's going to be a family holiday with just me and my daughter thank you!

Zombie: Fine! Pass me the phone, I'm gonna speak to *my* family!

Sarge: Pah! You haven't got a family... surely?

Zombie: Yes I have. I've got my mum, granny, my Scottish uncle, the twins...

Sarge: OK, what's their names? What's your mum called?

Zombie: Mummy zombie.

Sarge: Pah! And granny?

Zombie: Granny zombie.

Sarge: And the twins?

Zombie: The first one is called Zombie.

Sarge: ... and the second?

Zombie: Oww... it's on the tip of my tongue... erm... Oh yeah, Zombie.

Sarge: Hmmmn...

Zombie: And my Scottish uncle is Zombie Mc Zombie of the Mc Zombie clan...

Sarge: What a surprise...

Zombie: ...but we call him Googal McDougal - so as not to get confused.

Sarge: Of course, makes complete sense...

Zombie: Ahhh, it's going to be a great holiday, just the eight of us.

Sarge: No, no, no, no, no. Phone your family by all means, but you are NOT coming on holiday with us. Clear!?!

Zombie: Owww...

Narrator: Friday eventually arrives, Sarge packs the final bits into his daughter's van and both sit down to a cup of tea before setting off...

Daughter: Are you sure it's OK to leave the van unlocked whilst we sit here drinking tea daddy?

Sarge: Of course it is darling, only an idiot would try to get into a van parked outside a police station. Now drink up, I want to head off before Zombie sees us.

Daughter: Is that the new recruit that came to the hospital with you?

Sarge: Yes yes, but let's not ruin the holiday before it starts by talking about... work.

Daughter: I notice you're very 'tight lipped' when it comes to work issues - particularly about the new recruit. I know you can't say much about police work, but I am your daughter.

Sarge: Maybe I'll tell you a bit, once we're far away from this place, now let's get in the van shall we.

Narrator: Both get into the van and have a lovely catch up whilst driving.

Daughter: I've made a lovely picnic that I've put in the basket on the back seat. I've packed all your favourite foods and plenty of them, so we won't run out before we get there.

Sarge: Ooh goody goody, er...I mean...Oh good. By the way, how are the kittens?

Daughter: They're really lovely bless them. They've really grown since you saw them. And do you know, I think they chased a mouse into the van one time, because we left some shopping in it overnight once, and in the morning, most of the food packets had been eaten through!

Sarge: Oh my! Well, I'd better have some of the picnic now, just in case the mouse got away. Hehe.

Daughter: Oh dear, the sandwiches have been eaten.

Sarge: Oh well never mind, pass me a packet of crisps.

Daughter: They're all gone too. So are all the sausage rolls, quiche, cakes and salad. The only thing left is this apple, and that's been half eaten!

Sarge: OK, there's a service station in 10 miles, we'll pull into that, grab something to eat and see if we can find the mouse when there.

Daughter: That sounds like a plan. So, how's training the new recruit going? What's his name again?

Narrator: From under a blanket on the back seat: "Zombie."

Daughter: Zombie, that's right. You know, you really are good at ventriloquism. You should do more of that in your magic act because you made it sound like it came from under that tatty blanket of yours in the back seat.

Sarge: Eh, what are you on about? I thought you were using an old blanket to hide a mess from me. Anyway, in answer to your question, he's an idiot!

Zombie: No I'm not!

Sarge: Yes you are Zom...

Narrator: Sarge stops halfway through before continuing...

Sarge: Dear Lord no! Don't let it be...

Daughter: Are you OK? You've gone pale.

Sarge: Let's pull into the service station shall we... I think I might have discovered our 'mouse's' hiding place.

Narrator: Sarge pulls into the service station, gets out of the driver's seat, and opens the back door and speaks to the 'blanket'.

Sarge: My, you are a large mouse, it must be all that lovely picnic that made you that size. I'll have to get a very large stick to whack you with. Let me go and find one...

Zombie: No, no, no Sarge. It's really me, your friend Zombie.

Sarge: GET OUT!

Zombie: OK, OK.

Sarge: And if you think you're coming with us, you're very much mistaken.

Zombie: But I don't know how to get baaack.

Daughter: Daddy, we can't leave him here. I tell you what, you have all of the back seat area to yourself. I'll drive the rest of the way and have Zombie up front with me. When we get there, he can use the tent to camp in that I've got in the back, and we'll have the accommodation we've booked.

Sarge: Well, you're more generous than I'd be. As long as you're OK with him sitting up front with you? I'll have a nap.

Daughter: Yes, that's fine.

Zombie: Ooh goody goody. You are kind.

Daughter: That's OK.

Zombie: You are lovely.

Daughter: Thanks.

Zombie: You are pretty.

Daughter: Er… thank you.

Zombie: Are you a lady??

Daughter: Well, woman yes.

Zombie: Do you want a date?

Daughter: I did have some in the picnic basket, but you ate all of those…

Zombie: No, not that kind of date.

Daughter: Oh, you mean the other type. OK, how about 1066 - the Battle of Hastings?

Zombie: What?

Daughter: Agincourt 1415? The 1833 slavery abolition act? 1969 – first man on the moon…

Zombie: Stop it, you're making my head hurt with your Battle of Hashtags and man in the moon. I'm going to sleep.

Daughter: Good, 'cos that was getting a little creepy…

Narrator: Eventually they arrive, and Sarge's daughter drives around looking for their chalet...

Daughter: OK, wake up you two we're here. I just need to keep driving around until we find number 72...

Sarge: Well at least we got here without any more 'surprises'.

Zombie: Er... There is one more thing I need to tell you...

Narrator: Zombie sheepishly points to the back of the van where his family have been hiding under more blankets.

Family: Surprise!

Sarge: Zombie, as soon as this vehicle stops, I'm going to kick your...

Daughter: Ah, number 72. All out. Zombie, you show your family how to put up the tent and my dad and I will unpack and get the kettle on.

Zombie: Right you are Sarge's daughter.

Narrator: Sarge is making a cup of tea and he's looking out of the window at Zombie and his family whilst his daughter is unpacking.

Sarge: Look at them! The mother has got a saucepan on her head, granny has got knitting needles in her hair, the twins have got their coats on backwards, and they're all clanging pots and pans as they dance in a circle!!

Daughter: Oh let them be, maybe it's a family ritual or tradition where they come from...

Sarge: What - Mars!

Daughter: Oh daddy, stop it. Mind you, Zombie looked like he'd never seen a female before. He was being a bit inappropriate whilst you were asleep. I think he's got a crush on me.

Sarge: Really? Well, you'd better 'nip that in the bud' and tell him exactly what you think. Unfortunately, it's the only way he learns.

Daughter: Oh, I will. Looks like you're going to have to put up the tent for them. Send Zombie in whilst you're doing it.

Sarge: Zombie, my daughter wants a word with you. I'll put up the tent since none of you seem to have a clue.

Zombie: Do you think I should take my saucepan and wooden spoon with me?

Sarge: Oh yes. And if I were you, I'd wear it on your head...

Zombie: Oh yes, I want her to think of me as sophisticated.

Sarge: I was thinking more for protection!

Zombie: And Sarge, don't wait up. I think it's going to be a long night...

Daughter: Ah there you are Zombie. Can I borrow that wooden spoon?

Zombie: Sure, anything for *you*.

Daughter: Let me get one thing straight...

Narrator: Sarge's daughter proceeds to periodically hit the saucepan with the wooden spoon and a clang-a-lang-a-lang can be heard between her sentences...

Daughter: If you ever come on to me again, I'm going to...clang... then I'm going to get you by the...clang... and finally, I'll...clang... your...clang! Understood?

Zombie: Yessss!

Sarge: Ah Zombie, how was your date? Hehehehehehe.

Zombie: I can see where she gets it from, she's definitely **your** daughter!

Narrator: Both families are finally unpacked and settled into their own accommodation.

Sarge: Right, it is nearly bedtime, I'll just check on Zombie and his family.

Narrator: Sarge stands a little way away from where Zombie is sitting round a campfire with Granny and Googal.

Zombie: What do you see in the flames O mystical one?

Granny: Ooow, ooow, ooow, woah, woah, woah...

Zombie: What is it old crone? What hideous thing have you seen that makes you wail so??

Granny: It's my arthritis you idiot. And less is the old crone.

Zombie: Sorry Granny. Never mind, we shall have a reading from the ancient texts. Pray tell us a tale from the Mc Zombie clan.

Googal: Aye, I will. But I warn yea, it will send chills up your spine. For this is the tale of a creature with claws and sharp teeth...

Zombie: Claws and sharp teeth...

Googal: A creature that dressed - as a human...

Zombie: Dressed as a human...

Googal: Aye, and when he opened his mooth, all you could hear was...

Sarge: Zombie! Put that fire out! You know you shouldn't light a fire in the forest.

Zombie: It's only Sarge. We'll put the fire out once we've heard the rest of the gruesome tale of the creature who dressed as human.

Sarge: Well, I'll stay here to make sure you do!

Zombie: Alight, but be quiet, we're listening to stories from the old scriptures. Carry on.

Googal: As I was saying, the creature dressed as a human, even disguising himself with a hat on his head. But he could nae hide the fact that he had fur where flesh should be...

Zombie: Fur instead of flesh...

Googal: Aye, and he could nae hide the fact that he did not know our ways. For he'd been born in the deepest, darkest jungle of a foreign land.

Zombie: Deepest, darkest jungle.

Googal: Aye, and he'd gorge himself all day on the fruit of the marmarladey tree.

Sarge: Marmarladey??! Give me that book. Aha, just as I thought. This is the tale of Paddington bear, not an ancient script!

Googal: I'll have you know that book has been in our family for many, many years.

Sarge: I wouldn't be surprised; it's been overdue from the library for the last...27! Now go to bed the lot of you and I'll post this back to them in the morning.

Narrator*:* Sarge makes sure the fire is put out once they've gone to bed and goes to bed himself, ready for the next morning. In the morning, Sarge tells his daughter all about the previous night...

Daughter: ... and the book was actually Paddington you say? Well, don't get yourself wound-up, I noticed a hose pipe in the garden, so you can go and water the plants whilst I get ready, and we'll head off for our day out at the zip wire.

Sarge: That's a good idea, gardening always relaxes me.

Narrator: A while later, both are ready to go.

Daughter: Are we going to take…

Sarge: No! We are not! Besides, I didn't hear a peep coming from their tent, so hopefully they're all asleep. Come on, let's go.

Narrator: They arrive at their destination a while later.

Daughter: Are you sure I can't persuade you to try the zip wire? It'll be great fun.

Sarge: No flaming fear! It's killing me enough this steep walk up the mountain. I don't want to finish myself off by risking that. But you go ahead, I know how much you've been looking forward to it.

Narrator: As they near the top, a familiar face waves from the zip wire...

Zombie: Cooee Sarge. It's me Zombie. I'm with my family. Look.

Sarge: Oh God! How on earth did they get here??!

Daughter: And they've pushed their way to the front of the queue... And are getting on all at once!

Zombie: Weeeeeee...

Narrator: By the time Sarge and his daughter get to the top, staff are turning customers away...

Staff: Sorry Ladies and Gentlemen, the zip wire is now closed because a family ignored the safety rules, and all got on at once and snapped the zip wire.

Sarge: Sorry darling, I know you're upset, as this was the one thing you wanted to do on holiday. I tell you what, there's still the hot tub back at the chalet, I'll drive us back and pick up a bottle of wine and we'll sit in it and watch the sun go down.

Daughter: OK daddy, that sounds fine.

Narrator: (However, when they get back...)

Sarge: Oh... my... God, they've managed to get back before us and are in the hot tub. And look, mum is washing her pots and pans, Googal is having a bath... and you don't want to know what the twins are doing in it!!

Daughter: Did you only buy the one bottle of wine?

Sarge: Don't you worry about it, I'm already on it. You open the first one whilst I go out and buy more – and clear them out of the hot tub at the same time.

Narrator: A while later, whilst Sarge and his daughter are relaxing on the sofa, Googal knocks at the door.

Googal: Sorry to trouble you, but I wonder if I could borrow a glass of water to put out a wee fire?

Sarge: Fire? I thought I told Zombie not to light a fire in the forest?

Googal: Och no. We're a responsible family, we would nae let him play with matches. I lit the fire, but now we've cooked, I'm going to put it oot.

Sarge: Well, I still said not to have a fire in the forest.

Googal: Aye, I'm not daft… that's why I lit it in the tent.

Sarge: Oh good, you lit it in the…YOU LIT IT IN THE TENT!?

Googal: Aye, but there's no need to get cross because I cut a big hole in the roof to let the smoke out…

Daughter: I'll deal with this daddy since it's my tent. Googal, you go and show me the fire, and I'll get the hose…

Googal: Here it is wee lassie, now are you sure you know how to use a hose?

Daughter: Oh yes!

Googal: It's just that you're soaking me. Surely, you're meant to tackle the cause of the fire?

Daughter: YOU ARE THE CAUSE OF THE FIRE!

Googal: Well there's no need to shout.

Daughter: You're right. How about I make it up to you by buying you and your family choo-choo tickets to the station where the film of Paddington was shot?

Googal: Ooh goody Mc goody. Come on family, pack everything up. We're going on a long trip to that 'London' to see where they filmed the creature who dressed as a human.

Daughter: Right, I'll get the car packed and ready for us to take you.

Narrator: Sarge's daughter tells her dad of her plan and they eagerly pack. Sarge gets into the car after dropping the family at the station…

Daughter: Did they get on the train?

Sarge: I'm fairly sure they did, because it arrived pretty much as soon as I saw them get onto the platform. That's why I rushed back to the car, so we can drive off quickly. Oh blast, I forgot to post that book back. I'll nip and find a post box.

Daughter: Well, whilst you're doing that, I'll buy a lovely cake for the journey back home. That's enough holiday for me I'm afraid.

Narrator: Both returned to the car a few minutes later and chat on the way back about the holiday and other things.

Sarge: OK where's that cake you bought earlier?

Daughter: It's in that box on the back seat.

Sarge: it's been eaten!

Narrator: Sarge prods the blanket on the back seat. Zombie has *somehow* managed to escape his family and sneaked into the car once again. He makes a pathetic attempt to sound like a mouse...

Zombie: Squeak, squeak??

Sarge/Daughter: ZOMBIE!

Zombie goes to Therapy   S1 E10

Chief Inspector: Ah Spicer, just the man. We need to use up our budget before the end of the financial year, so thought we'd spend it on something constructive to the force.

Sarge: You mean a nice meal out!

Chief Inspector: Not quite, but something for staff well-being.

Sarge: A holiday?

Chief Inspector: No... therapy.

Sarge: Therapy!?

Chief Inspector: Yes... therapy.

Sarge: Ah, of course, for Zombie you mean... straighten him out.

Chief Inspector: No, both of you...together.

Sarge: Good Lord no!

Chief Inspector: Yes, it will be very good for morale. You ring this number and arrange a session for both of you and I'll find Zombie and tell him.

Sarge: Right you are Chief Inspector.

Narrator: Zombie comes grinning towards Sarge after hearing the news.

Zombie: Here, guess what Sarge...? We're going to therapy... together... as a couple.

Sarge: A couple means 2, and as our budget only stretches to two people, Chief Inspector chose the two that work together the most.

Zombie: Owww... Still, Chief Inspector thought it would improve our morals.

Sarge: Morale you idiot! That means well-being to you.

Zombie: Owww... And what's therapy?

Sarge: It's where one nutcase tells another nutcase what's wrong with them, but the psychiatrist - gets paid for it! But we won't be going to a psychiatrist, we'll be going to a counsellor to talk about our problems.

Zombie: Oh good, I'll tell them about the bins and the roads.

Sarge: Why on earth would you tell them about your bins and the roads?

Zombie: Because a counsellor works for the council!

Sarge: A counsellor, not a councillor!

Zombie: That's what I said.

Sarge: A couns...never mind. You know, you're the reason they limit session to an hour. The counsellor we're seeing – Dr Franks, will need to spend a whole year just on working you out! And don't you embarrass me tomorrow when we go. Don't do anything daft when were there. And for God's sake, smarten yourself up!

Zombie: Right you are Sarge.

Sarge: And Zombie, go and get a haircut - you look a right state!

Zombie: Right you are Sarge.

Narrator: Zombie goes off to get a haircut, whilst Sarge fills in an online questionnaire for their session. Zombie then returns.

Sarge: I thought I told you to get a haircut?!

Zombie: I did. I got this one at the front cut. The barber even put it in this plastic bag to prove he'd cut my hair.

Sarge: Well, he must have poor eyesight if he thinks that's a haircut.

Zombie: Actually, he's got really good eyesight!

Sarge: Really? How do you work that out then?

Zombie: Because when I asked him why it cost £200, he said because he saw me coming from a mile away!

Sarge: You paid £200!

Zombie: Actually, he did it for nothing when I told him I worked for the police.

Sarge: I bet he did! Anyway, you have to fill out this online form before we see counsellor Franks.

Zombie: Right you are Sarge.

Narrator: Dr Franks has read their online questionnaires by the time of their session, and he greets them at his office.

Franks: Velcome bose of you, I'm Dr. Franks, do come in.

Zombie: Hello Dr Frankenstein, I'm Zombie and this is my sergeant who's called Sarge.

Sarge: Actually, it's Sergeant Terry Spicer.

Franks: Right you are Mr Spicer, sit down. You too Zombie - take a seat.

Zombie: Ooh, thank you very much.

Franks: Zombie, why are you taking zat chair out of my office?

Zombie: Because you said take a seat Dr Frankfurter.

Franks: 'Take a seat' means to sit down.

Zombie: Owww...

Franks: So, as you know, I usually do family and couples' counselling. But I can do some vork viz you around vork relationships if you choose to go beyond zis initial session. I have an idea from your online responses what you need individual vork on.

Sarge: Oh yes? And what's that?

Franks: For you Mr Spicer...it is your emotional intelligence and understanding others. For you Zombie, you need a lot of vork on... your intelligence... And understanding... well... anything!

Zombie: What do you mean?

Franks: Take your first answer to the question: "what are you hoping to get when you come to therapy?" You answered - post it notes. Your answer to the question: "what do you know about therapy?" Was banana, bicycle, underpants. And your answer to question 3 was "flubjigaboo"!

Zombie: The button got stuck on the keyboard with that one!

Sarge: See what I have to put up with!!

Zombie: Well, at least I only have to do half of what Dr Frankly says you need to do.

Sarge: How do you work that one out??

Zombie: Because you have to work on emotional intelligence, and I only have to work on the 'intelligence' half of that.

Sarge: Why you little...

Narrator: Dr Franks has to pull Sarge off of Zombie and decides to do the session in two parts.

Franks: OK zat is enough. I think it'll work better if I do your sessions in two halves. Mr Spicer, you go and relax in reception whilst I speak to Zombie. Zen, halfway through, you and I vill chat. There are some nice Disneyland and holiday brochures to flick through for relaxing holiday ideas.

Sarge: Thank you, yes, that sounds good.

Franks: Now Zombie, apart from just now, how do you and Mr Spicer get along?

Zombie: He moans at me a lot. "Zombie, don't eat those crayons." "Zombie, don't swing that boiled kettle around your head." "Zombie, stop flicking the light switch on and off." "Zombie, focus on what I've asked you to do..."

Franks: I see. Sorry, could I get you to sit down instead of hanging from my ceiling fan?

Zombie: Look at me, I'm on a merry-go-round. Weeeeeeeeeee.

Franks: I'm glad you're enjoying your session, but it gets very hot in here wizout zat fan vorking. So please get off... before it breaks. There's a good chap.

Zombie: Ooh, can we go and feed the penguins? Please, please, please.

Franks: Penguins? There are no penguins.

Zombie: Yes there are. Those big ones, over the road when you look out of your window.

Narrator: Dr Franks looks out of his window and realises what Zombie means.

Franks: Ahh, I see what you mean. Yes, I suppose with their outfits being black and white, they do look like penguins. But those are nuns and that is a monastery over the road. The Garden of Tranquilly is open to the public if you wanted to visit after your session? But proper penguins are small, you don't get animals the size of humans.

Zombie: Yes you do!

Franks: No you don't!

Zombie: OK, so how come there's a giant mouse and a giant duck on the front cover of one of those magazines in reception then?

Franks: Zat is Mickey Mouse and Donald duck you id... you... you.

Zombie: Owww, the merry-go-round has stopped. The 50p must have run out. You got any more in your desk drawer?

Franks: Do you mind not just going through my drawers, zat is rude.

Narrator: Zombie isn't listening as usual, and every time Dr Franks closes one drawer - Zombie opens another...

Zombie: You must have 50p somewhere...

Franks: It doesn't run on money, now leave that drawer alone!

Zombie: There must be a button to start the merry-go-round up then...

Narrator: Zombie climbs all over the desk trying to open drawers. Papers go flying, Dr Franks is getting tied up in the telephone cord as he's trying to phone through to his secretary - whilst also fighting Zombie off from being a pest.

Franks: You're a nosy little... Sharon, sank goodness you answered, could you take my client for a valk whilst I spend the second half of zee session with Mr Spicer? Sank you.

Narrator: Sharon leads Zombie out and Dr Franks invites Sarge in.

Sarge: Oh my, is this mess in your office something to do with Zombie?

Franks: Don't worry about zee mess, Zombie chose to have an 'active' session, zat's all. Erm... do you mind if we have zee vindow open during your session, it's just zee fan has stopped vorking and it gets hot in here otherwise.

Sarge: Well as long as any outside noise doesn't stop us from hearing each other, or being able to think?

Franks: No, no, no. Nothing of the sort. In all my years of vorking here all you hear is the sound of birdsong and the gentle trickle of zee fountain. It's most peaceful actually.

Sarge: Go ahead then, that sounds lovely. Now, what did you want to talk about?

Franks: Well, I'm getting quite a good idea of what Zombie must be like to vork with. So, let's talk about you. What was life like growing up? Tell me about your parents...

Sarge: Well, my dad was an army man. Very disciplined, wouldn't stand for any nonsense. Liked things nice and orderly. Used to buy me soldiers for every birthday but would only let me play with them if I played quietly... and put them away... neatly.

Franks: I see, and your mother?

Sarge: Oh no, she never played with soldiers.

Franks: No, I mean what was she like!?

Sarge: Oh, I see. Ah, she was a very patient woman.

Franks: And how did she and your father get on?

Sarge: Pretty well... I think. The only time I saw them argue is when she bought me a magic set for Christmas instead of more... soldiers.

Franks: You smiled when you said magic set, why is zat?

Sarge: Aah magic, I love to talk about...

Narrator: Just at that moment, Sarge is interrupted by a large 'splash' followed by a scream and then general pandemonium coming from outside...

Franks: Dear Lord, somebody has thrown one of the nuns into the fountain.

Sarge: Oh God! It's HIM isn't it!! Sorry Dr Franks, I've got to go...

Narrator: As Sarge leaves, Dr Frank's secretary enters. Her hair is in a mess and she's very flustered.

Sharon: Dr Franks, sorry to disturb you, but I think we need to call the police. That client you asked me to take for a walk is picking up the nuns and putting them in the water saying that's where they belong. Then he stole my tuna sandwiches and tried to feed them to them.

Narrator: Both watch out of the window helplessly as a figure is chased by a bunch of nuns shaking their fists. All they can hear is a: "Ooh hoo hoo hoo" as the figure runs into the chapel...

Franks: It used to be such a quiet neighbourhood...

Sharon: There, there Dr Franks. I'll make you a nice cup of tea.

Narrator: Sharon goes off and the chapel bell can be heard ringing. Doctor Franks looks out of the window to see Zombie swinging on the bell. 'Dong, Dong, Dong, Dong'... The bell strikes 13 times and is soon drowned out by the sirens of all three emergency services. By the time Sharon returns, Dr Franks is slumped below the window, a quivering mess, with a twitching eye talking to himself.

Franks: Heehee, 13 o'clock, yes that's about right. Haha, swinging on a bell. Like Quasimodo... hmmm,

hmmm, hmmm, hahahaha. Pushing nuns into a fountain, trying to feed them like ducks, hmmm hmmm hahaha. Going through my desk and thinking my fan is a merry-go-round...Hahahaha.

Sharon: There, there Dr Franks. Have a cup of tea to calm your nerves. Do you want me to cancel your final appointment of the day?

Franks: No no. I'll be alright, I'm a professional. Haha, heehee.

Sharon: Are you sure, they are in reception, I could tell them to re-book?

Franks: No no, it's fine. It'll be nice to see a family group. After all, no client could ever be a vorse experience than zee one we've just had! Tell zem I'll be 10 minutes.

Sharon: Dr Franks said he'll be 10 minutes, he's just having a cup of tea, then he'll be right with you.

Googal: Ooh goody Mc goody! Did you hear that family? The man who can see into your head will soon be with us. I bet he's really looking forward to meeting us all. I can't wait to see his face...

Zombie Turns to Crime   S1 E11

Narrator: Sarge is on the phone to Chief Inspector.

Sarge: Aha, yes, I see, aha yes, keep it hush-hush? Will do Chief Inspector. Bye.

Zombie: Who was that, Sarge?

Sarge: Never you mind.

Zombie: It was Chief Inspector... and you and him are planning something and he told you to keep it hush-hush from Zombie. Keep what hush-hush from me??

Sarge: Oh, that we are planning a surpri...NEVER YOU MIND!

Zombie: FINE!

Narrator: Zombie storms out of the police station - slamming the door behind him.

PC Smith: What's the matter with Zombie, Sarge?

Sarge: Oh, he's annoyed I wouldn't tell him about the surprise we're planning for when he's finished his probation period.

PC Smith: Do you really think he'll make it as a policeman?

Sarge: Pah! I've got more chance of becoming the king of England. But Chief Inspector says if he doesn't do anything daft over the next few weeks, he'll pass his probation. Apparently, it's the thing he wants most in the world - to become a policeman.

PC Smith: Really? When I asked him what he'd like most in the world - he said 5 post it notes!

Sarge: Pah, well there you go then!

PC Smith: He then changed his mind…

Sarge: Oh, then he decided he'd like to be a policeman, did he?

PC Smith: No… he said chocolate cake.

Narrator: Just then the phone rings…

Sarge: Ah Mr McGurk… yes yes. What? Someone came storming through the allotment and pulled up loads of plants? Then they did **what** to your wife when she was bent over? But she can't give a description because her head got stuck in a pot! He put his hands on her bottom and pushed her over?! Well, can you give me a description? A great, big hideous thing? No, I meant a description of the perpetrator... oh, that was what you were describing! Oh... well OK, I'll put people on alerts then. Goodbye.

PC Smith: What was that about McGurk's wife Sarge?

Sarge: Oh, that some idiot has pushed her over when she was bending over.

PC Smith: What kind of idiot would dare do that to Mrs McGurk?

Sarge: I've got an idea what kind of idiot would! I'm going to write this up. Can you send Zombie in to see me when he returns?

PC Smith: Right you are Sarge.

Narrator: A bit later Zombie returns.

Zombie: PC Smith says you want a word with me Sarge?

Sarge: Yes I do, and you can drop the 'attitude'. Were you at the allotments earlier?

Zombie: No!

Sarge: I know you're lying Zombie, and I'll tell you how I know.

Zombie: How?

Sarge: You've got mud all over your hands and shoes. You've got a flower sticking out of your back pocket. AND YOU'VE GOT MRS. McGURK'S HAT ON!

Zombie: Owww...

Sarge: Furthermore, you grabbed hold of her bottom to push her over.

Zombie: Well, the great big things in my way!

Sarge: No, no, no, no, no, no, no. I don't want to hear your excuses. My daughter has already told you about being inappropriate when it comes to women, when you were pestering her during our holiday. Remember?

Zombie: Yesss. But she's not a policeman!

Sarge: You don't need to be a policeman to know if something is wrong or right, and even if you're not a human, you should know by now, you do not act inappropriately nor touch someone inappropriately.

Zombie: Can I touch their...

Sarge: NO! And certainly not there... on anybody! If you did that, you would spend a *long* time in prison!

Zombie: What - 10 minutes??

Sarge: Pah! 10 minutes! Oh…to you Zombie - that probably is a long time. No -10 years more likely.

Zombie: FINE! I'll spend 10 years in prison for touching her bottom.

Sarge: If you apologise to her and give her her hat back, she might not take it any further.

Zombie: No, you said I've got to go to jail for 10 years, so I'll put myself in prison then. Good bye!

Narrator: Zombie goes into the cells and slams the door on himself.

Sarge: Zombie, that's not what I said, and you know it. You're just still cross from this morning because I wouldn't tell you what Chief Inspector and I discussed.

Zombie: No… yes. Has it been 10 years yet though?

Sarge: 37 seconds actually.

Zombie: PC Smith, PC Smith! I'm being held against my will, call the police, call Amnesty International, call my solicitor!

PC Smith: What's going on Sarge?!

Sarge: As usual, Zombie is being daft. He has voluntarily put himself in prison, rather than face up to Mrs McGurk.

PC Smith: Oh, I see. And what's this about a solicitor?

Sarge: Take no notice, he doesn't need one, and if he says he's got one, it'll be a mad family member.

Zombie: Actually, I use the firm Googal McDougal and Right-Noodle.

Sarge: Oh God - his uncle. PC Smith, ring his uncle and see if he can talk sense into him.

PC Smith: Right you are Sarge.

Narrator: A little while later, Googal turns up at the police station.

Googal: Good afternoon, Sergeant Spicy, I'm here to see my client.

Sarge: Ah, I see by the book you're carrying you've been reading up on the law. What is it this time... 'Googal's big book of nursery crimes'? Pahahahaha.

Googal: No comment.

Sarge: Anyway, do you think you can talk some sense into him?

Googal: No comment.

Sarge: Stop being daft. 'No comment' is what you are meant to tell your client to say, surely?

Googal: No comment.

Sarge: Bah. Anyway, he's this way. Do you want a cup of tea?

Googal: No comment.

Zombie: Is that you Googal?

Googal: No comment Zombie.

Narrator: Sarge opens the cell door and leaves them to it and has a cup of tea with PC Smith before going into the village. When he returns, Zombie and Googal are still in the cell...

Sarge: Have they been in there all this time??

PC Smith: Yes Sarge. I didn't want to disturb a private conversation.

Sarge: Well, I'm going to see what they're up to...

Narrator: As Sarge heads to the cell door, he can hear Zombie's voice…

Zombie: Aeroplane? Computer? Elephant?

Googal: No, do you give up?

Zombie: Yes.

Googal: It was Zombie. Z for Zombie!

Narrator: Sarge swings the door open full of rage…

Sarge: OUT you get Googal. I didn't invite you here to play 'I spy'! And as for you Zombie, you can stay in the cells for all I care, it's your annual leave you're wasting, not mine!

Googal: Fine, I'll go!

Zombie: Fine, I'll stay!

Sarge: Fine, I'll have a cup of tea!

Zombie: Yeah, I'll have a cup of tea too Sarge. And for my takeaway tonight, I'll have burger and chips, a big bottle of coke and an ice cream.

Sarge: Oh no Zombie, hardened criminals like you don't get take away! Do they PC Smith?

PC Smith: No Sarge, they get prison food and a lukewarm tea, at best.

Sarge: Yes, we'll just have to have Zombie's takeaway ourselves, and if we can't eat it all tonight, put it in the fridge for breakfast. But ask again in 10 years Zombie. Night.

Zombie: Fine, see if I care! Good… night!

Narrator: One week later…

PC Smith: How long has Zombie been in the cells now Sarge?

Sarge: A week! And all because he refuses to write a letter of apology to Mrs McGurk.

PC Smith: Can he *actually* write Sarge?

Sarge: Well, I offered for him to record it on a dictaphone, but he still refused, so I bet he's actually still cross about me not telling him about the surprise we're planning - rather than Mrs McGurk.

PC Smith: Blimey!

Sarge: He'll be in for a surprise in a bit though, Upper Ringclay want us to hold Keith Averley while they investigate him.

PC Smith: Old 'Keith the thief'! What's he been up to now?

Sarge: We caught him acting suspiciously around the post office. He's bound to be planning something.

PC Smith: So, you think chucking him in with Zombie will help?

Sarge: One of two things will happen. Either Zombie will be frightened into giving up his protest because a REAL criminal is in the cell...

PC Smith: Or?

Sarge: Or, 'Keith the thief' will be driven so mad by Zombie, he'll beg us to get him out of the cell!

PC Smith: The last option sounds more likely!

Sarge: We're about to find out. 'Keith the thief' is here...

Narrator: 'Keith the thief' is processed and led to the cells...

Sarge: Here you go Zombie, meet your new cellmate, Keith.

Zombie: Hi, my name's Zombie, what's your name?

Keith: Are you a bit stupid, he's just told you it's Keith!

Zombie: OK OK, no need to raise your voice, you sound like my boss Sarge when you speak like that.

Keith: You're a copper!?

Zombie: Well, training to be one, but Sarge doesn't trust me to do anything. So, I make tea mainly.

Narrator: Keith listens to Zombie for a while and soon realises he might be able to trick him into doing what he wants.

Keith: Well, if I was your boss, I'd treat you really kindly and let you have whatever you wanted. And let you be in charge of things.

Zombie: What, you'd give me some pink post it notes?

Keith: Ha hur hur, is that what you really... yeah, yeah of course you could have those, you're my mate after all. Funny enough, where I work, there's loads of those.

Zombie: Ooh ooh what's your job?

Keith: I'm a thie... security guard for the post office. Yeah, I was on my way there tonight when Sergeant Pepper mistook me for a criminal. I'm a bit forgetful see, and I forgot to wear my uniform.

Zombie: Ow, that's mean of him.

Keith: Yeah, then he called me stupid because I couldn't remember how much money was in the safe.

Zombie: Well, £20,572 is hard to remember.

Keith: Cor blimey! You're really good at remembering numbers. I bet you can tell me the 6-digit code to the safe...

Zombie: Sorry, Sarge told me never to tell people.

Keith: No no, of course not. And if it was me, I'd trick them by telling them *double* the real answer.

Zombie: Well, I couldn't do that, 'cos I don't know what double 150907 is.

Keith: Ha hur hur. We ought to work out a way of escaping from this cell - tonight. So... I can go to my job, and you can show Sergeant Salty how clever you really are. You don't want him to call you stupid, do you?

Zombie: Wellll, the joke would be on him then, because all the time I've been in jaaail, I've had the spare keeey.

Keith: You've been in jail a week - and all this time you've had a key to get out!! You really are a pr...etty clever person. C'mon, Let's go. But if you're going to help me in my job, you've got to wear a mask and gloves. Because of er... COVID.

Zombie: Right you are Keith.

Keith: And when we get there, you've got the important job of opening the bags, while I put the money in. Then we have to take it to a safe house in the countryside, so no robbers can get it.

Zombie: Right you are Keith.

Narrator: Whilst Zombie and 'Keith the thief' are in the post office, a silent alarm has been triggered at the police station and Sarge goes to the post office to investigate...

Sarge: Hello? Hello? Is there somebody there?

Keith: Oh God it's your Sarge, we'll have to work out how to get rid of him...

Zombie: Don't worry about it. I've got a clever trick to get rid of him. Watch... "There are not two people hiding in here, this is a recording made on a... made on a..."

Sarge: Dictaphone?!

Zombie: Yes, that's right, on a dictaphone.

Sarge: Aha, I know who's there!

Keith: Quick, bonk him on the head, so he doesn't remember who he saw when he wakes up.

Narrator: Zombie gives a timid tap on the head that has no effect, so Keith does it hard enough to render Sarge unconscious.

Zombie: Ooh hoo hoo hoo, I think you've killed him. He's going to be so cross!

Keith: Well, you did it first, so you'll be in trouble too. You'll get a good bash from me if you tell anyone, so let's get out of here before they catch us.

Narrator: Sarge wakes up with a sore head and is treated in hospital then released - as it's not as bad as first thought.

PC Smith: I'm sorry you got bashed and can't remember what happened. Forensics reckons it's an inside job because the safe wasn't damaged. One strange thing about it though, was all the pink post it notes were taken... strange. Oh, and I don't mean to be the bearer of more bad news, but when I came in this morning - the cells were empty.

Sarge: Oh God, that's all I need.

PC Smith: You take it easy for the next couple of days Sarge, I'll deal with everything - don't you worry.

Sarge: OK, if you want me, I'll be in my bed.

Narrator: A few days pass with PC Smith in charge when Sarge comes down - fully recovered.

Sarge: Morning PC Smith, I feel as right as rain, thank you for taking over for a while. Any news on the post office job?

PC Smith: Not really Sarge. They reckon the villains must be lying low somewhere in the Ringclay area.

Sarge: Talking of little villains, any news on Keith or Zombie?

PC Smith: No Sarge. They're working on the theory that Keith kidnapped Zombie... for some reason.

Sarge: Pah, 'Keith the thief' would rather turn himself in then spend time being driven nuts.

PC Smith: Talking about being driven nuts...

Sarge: Oh God Googal, what do you want??

Googal: Good morning, Sergeant Spice rack. I hope you're treating my client well whilst he's in your custody?

Sarge: No comment!

Googal: Be like that if you will. I've dropped in to let you know, I've started up a petition to free Zombie from his unlawful imprisonment.

Sarge: Pah, only other criminals and idiots would sign that!

Googal: I'll have you know; I've been to every household in the Ringclay area to get signatures. And I'll tell yea... I've got quite a few.

Sarge: Pah, give me that... Just as I thought. Family member... family member... family member. How many *actual* members of the public?

Googal: Ooh, let me see now... there was...oh and then there was... Oh yes - who can forget...

Sarge: How many!?!

Googal: ... 1.

Sarge: What, *this* scribble at the bottom?

Googal: Aye!

Sarge: Name – Z. Address - Baddies Hideout, Brick Kiln Farm, Muggeridge Lane. HOLD ON! Did you actually *speak* to this person??

Googal: Aye...

Sarge: And did they... by any chance... look like Zombie?!

Googal: Hehe, Funny you should mention that, if I didn't know he was in your cell, I'd have thought the same. I even told him he looked like Zombie. And he told me hehehe - I looked like his uncle Googal!! Ooh, hehehehe ooh - We did have a laugh!! Anyway, good day.

Sarge: Not a braincell between them. PC Smith, I'm off to Brick Kiln Farm. Send back up will you. I might be about to solve the mystery of the 'missing cons'.

PC Smith: Right you are Sarge.

Narrator: Sarge gets to the old farmhouse and peers through the dusty windows. Inside, most of the furniture is covered in sheets - as if no one has lived there for a long time. At a table however, a familiar figure can be seen counting post it notes. Sarge

decides to pull a prank on Zombie, so creeps up behind him, with a sheet over his head like a ghost...

Zombie: 1,2...er... 1,2...7? No. 1,2...ow - a million... I'm rich beyond my wildest dreams!!

Sarge: Woo hoo hoooo, it's a pity you had to kill someone to get rich Zombie. I'm going to haunt you for the rest of your liiife, unless you confess to what you've been up to...

Zombie: I'm s...sorry Sarge's ghost. We didn't mean to kill you when we bonked you on the head.

Sarge: Then you'd better tell me everything you know - right from the beginning...

Zombie: Mary had a little lamb...

Sarge: Not that far back you id... I mean woohoohoo, not that far baaack. Everything you know from the day you pushed Mrs McGurk over...

Zombie: Well, the 'alive' Sarge had annoyed me because he wouldn't tell me what he was planning, so I deliberately pushed her over by touching her bottom and I stole her hat. I knew it was wrong but didn't want to admit it. Then, when I went to the cells, I took the spare keeey – so I could sneak out to get the leftover takeaway in friiidge.

Sarge: Oh, that was you! PC Smith and I thought Mrs Buckle must have chucked it out. Carry on...

Zombie: Then, when Keith was put in the cell, he told me he was a security guard, but you were stopping him from going to work. And if I helped him to get out, he'd take me to work with him - and I could have as many post it notes as I wanted as payment. I've always wanted to be a security guard see ghosty.

Sarge: And I suppose if you worked with a queen, you would have always wanted to have been a royal, or a spaceman if you met an astronaut.

Zombie: Oh yeah dead Sarge, that's a good idea...

Narrator: Sarge has had enough and throws off the sheet.

Sarge: Right, that's enough of this nonsense, I'm not dead and you're not a very good criminal...or policemen. And you won't make your probation when Chief Inspector finds out what you've been up to and where Keith and the money is. Get in the back of the police car. We're off to the nick.

Zombie: What was it like when you were a ghost, Sarge? I've always wanted to be a ghost...

Sarge: Zombie, if you don't stop talking all the way there, I'll be very tempted to make your wish come true!

Zombie: Right you are Sarge.

Zombie's Hard Work   S1E12

Narrator: Zombie and Sarge are in the car on the way to the nick.

Sarge: You really are an idiot Zombie!

Zombie: I'll have you know; I have the brain of a clever person.

Sarge: Well, you'd better give it back - before they notice.

Zombie: Yes, I have thoughts what are clever.

Sarge: It's a pity then, you don't let those thoughts escape.

Zombie: If you had a dog what was clever and could do tricks, you wouldn't let him escape, would you?

Sarge: Hmmmn, true I suppose. But you actually know nothing!

Zombie: Yes I do! Ask me to tell you what I know about someone clever.

Sarge: OK, what do you know about Einstein and his 'theory of relativity'?

Zombie: That's easy. Gilbert Einstein came up with the 'theory of relatives'. He came up with the theory that: where there's a will - there's a relative!

Sarge: Pah! Although true... in a way. What about his 'special theory'?

Zombie: Gilbert Einstein's 'special theory' was *special* because he only got it out at Christmas - when his relatives came round.

Sarge: You do talk absolute poppycock. OK, what about **Albert** Einstein?

Zombie: Albert Einstein was Gilbert's little brother. He never amounted to anything. He was always getting into trouble at school because he insisted on writing his DJ name MC squared everywhere. He did have some minor success on the rave scene, but this was short lived, due to him selling drugs.

Sarge: What absolute nonsense!

Zombie: It's true, my mate Barry told me. The police kept seeing the tag $E = MC$ squared everywhere. They were baffled for ages until someone with Police Intelligence worked out the Ecstasy is known as E on the rave scene. And because they knew MC squared was Albert Einstein's DJ name, they worked out that $E = MC$ squared...was where to get drugs.

Sarge: Nonsense. E equals energy in the equation E = MC squared.

Zombie: Exactly! What does Ecstasy give you? Energy!

Sarge: Your mate Barry sounds as daft as you.

Zombie: He's not as daft as me, he's really clever! He can eat a banana without peeling it!

Sarge: Really? And how does he do that??

Zombie: His... his mum peels it for him.

Sarge: Idiot!

Zombie: Ooh ooh Sarge, look! There's a flock of cows in that field!

Sarge: Herd!

Zombie: Heard of what?

Sarge: Herd of cows.

Zombie: Of course I've heard of cows. There's a flock of them in that field!

Sarge: Oh God.

Zombie: It's a laugh, isn't it Sarge?

Sarge: What's a laugh?

Zombie: That noise that comes out of your mouth when you find something funny.

Sarge: Zombie, I'd stop making silly comments or... jokes - if that's what you call them. You're in enough trouble as it is.

Zombie: Am I going to go to jail for REAL this time Sarge?

Sarge: That depends on a lot of things...

Zombie: Like what?

Sarge: You don't need to know, but firstly we've got to find 'Keith the thief' and the money.

Zombie: Well, you won't get it out of me!

Sarge: Get *what* out of you?

Zombie: That 'Keith the thief' is hiding in the barn at the back of the farm, in the hayloft... oops!

Sarge: Oh really!

Zombie: Yeah...but at least I didn't tell you he's buried the money 3 foot from the front of the farmhouse to the left of the tree!

Sarge: Thank you very much Zombie, I'll radio PC Smith to let him know.

Narrator: Sarge radios PC Smith and puts Zombie in the cells - checking him for keys before doing so! PC

Smith returns to the station with the money and 'Keith the thief' and books him in.

PC Smith: There you go Sarge - Keith Averley and all of the money - every single penny!

Sarge: Well done Smith. Didn't want to spend any of your ill-gotten gains then Keith?

Keith: I didn't have a bloody chance! Every time I went somewhere, that Zombie guy would follow me, pestering me to get him a takeaway, or help him count his post it notes. And when he wasn't doing that, he'd asked me daft questions like: "Is the moon made out of cheese?" or "How many blades of grass are they in the world?" I'm glad to be rid of him!

Sarge: Oh yes, that's Zombie alright. I almost feel sorry for you. To make up for it, I've got a nice surprise for you…

Keith: You have?!

Sarge: Oh yes…

Narrator: Sarge opens the cell door…

Zombie: Hi, my name is Zombie, what's…

Keith: Oh no, please Sergeant Spicer, anything but that!! I'll do anything you want, please, please, please...

Sarge: Well, when you're ready to confess, let us know. But for now, you'll have to stay here until Upper Ringclay collect you!

Narrator: Sarge closes the cell door and all you can hear is Keith wailing...

PC Smith: Upper Ringclay have just phoned Sarge; to say they'll take Keith by the end of the day. And Chief Inspector left a message to say he'll come to see you tomorrow morning - about Zombie.

Sarge: OK PC Smith, but tell Upper Ringclay to take their time, no rush. Pahaha.

PC Smith: He'll be singing like a canary by the time they arrive!

Sarge: Exactly!

Narrator: Keith is taken away that night and Chief Inspector arrives in the morning. Only he and Sarge are at the station.

Chief Inspector: Well, I must congratulate you and PC Smith Spicer, for cracking the case. He's admitted to everything and several crimes we weren't aware of! How did you get him to confess?

Sarge: Well, ironically, Zombie had a hand in that. Talking of 'you know who', what are we going to *do* about him?

Chief Inspector: Well, luckily enough, we're covered legally, because as part of a plea-bargain, Keith begged us not to let anyone know that he needed Zombie to help him. Didn't want the embarrassment, I guess.

Sarge: More like he didn't want to end up in the same prison together! Either way, he won't pass his probation now and won't be able to stay here... surely?

Chief Inspector: Shall we have a brew and discuss that?

Sarge: Good idea, I'll put the kettle on...

Narrator: Sarge goes to the kitchen whilst Chief Inspector carries on talking...

Chief Inspector: The *boffins* will obviously need a report on him, as they're thinking he might need some further education and maybe experience of other jobs -

to see how zombies integrate in the wider world. How's he getting on?

Narrator: Chief Inspector makes his way to the kitchen after asking this...

Sarge: He's getting on my t...tea, Chief Inspector?

Chief Inspector: No, coffee for me Spicer please. Let's review how he's done so far...

Sarge: The first night he was here, he locked us both in the cell.

Chief Inspector: Ah, but he did catch that mugger.

Sarge: Not before locking himself to a drainpipe!

Chief Inspector: What about him representing the police and winning a prize for us at the village fete? Or that extremely funny magic show you assisted him with. You know, the one you pretended you couldn't do your escapology act?

Sarge: Let's not even talk about that shall we. What about the £5000 it cost when he burned down the police station?

Chief Inspector: Actually, he's been quite cost-effective - according to the petty-cash records. Look - plus £7390.40.

Sarge: Minus £7390.40, actually. Zombie altered the minus sign if you look closely.

Chief Inspector: Oh... so his record here has been a mixture of pluses and minuses - if you pardon the pun. So, on balance then, his creators are probably right to see how he does when 'left to his own devices'.

Sarge: When you say: 'left to his own devices', you don't mean...

Chief Inspector: No, no, no, no, no. He'll have plenty of like-minded people around him to help him and guide him. He'll try out different jobs and hobbies and be educated. He'll be looked after.

Sarge: Oh good.

Chief Inspector: You have a soft spot for him, don't you?

Sarge: No! Yes. I just want him to do well...

Chief Inspector: And return one day?

Sarge: Don't push it Chief Inspector. I'll see you when it's all arranged. Goodbye.

Chief Inspector: Goodbye Spicer and congratulations once again on all of your good work.

Narrator: The day finally comes when Zombie has to leave. Sarge has boxed up all of his 'stuff' and Chief Inspector is waiting in a car outside...

Zombie: Sarge, do I have to go? I promise I won't do anything daft or silly ever again. I'll be really quiet and won't annoy you. Please, please, please. You wouldn't have to pay me.

Sarge: You'd have to work for nothing... with all the damage you've caused!

Zombie: So, can I stay then!?

Sarge: No! Er... I mean no Zombie; they want you to complete your second *phase* now...

Zombie: Owww...

Sarge: But PC Smith and I have clubbed together to get you a few things for your new place. Bring out the presents PC smith. Bring the white box first PC smith.

PC Smith: Right you are Sarge.

Sarge: Now in this box...

Zombie: Was a chocolate cake.

Sarge: Yes! How did you kn... you ate it didn't you!

Zombie: No! Yeees.

Sarge: Well, we also got you...

Zombie: An Xbox, 2 controllers and some games.

Sarge: Oh I see, so you've opened those as well? Still got to work on your patience I see Zombie.

Zombie: Yep. Right, you got any more presents, or can I go now?

Sarge: Actually, I do have one more that you haven't managed to open because I kept it on me. Here you go Zombie.

Zombie: Bit small, isn't it?

Sarge: Hmmmn.

Narrator: Zombie opens it and is genuinely excited and pleased.

Zombie: Ooh goody goody. Pink post it notes - my favourite. Thank you, Sarge.

Sarge: That's alright Zombie… but why are you now holding them up to the light??

Zombie: Got to check for forgeries - you never know in this day and age!

Sarge: Why you little…

PC Smith: Right, I think Chief Inspector has waited long enough Zombie, let's get all of your stuff into the car, shall we?

Narrator: The car is packed, and Zombie is in the back seat.

Zombie: Will you come and see me at my new place Sarge?

Sarge: Well… I…er….

Zombie: Please…

Narrator: Sarge has to turn away as the car drives off. Zombie looking out of the back window…

… Chief Inspector and Zombie arrive at the new place…

Chief Inspector: Right, this is your new place Zombie. I'll introduce you to Sergio later who runs the place and will help you with everything you need.

Zombie: What, isn't Sarge going to be here every day, telling me what to do?

Chief Inspector: No, no, no Zombie. He'll be busy running the police station, remember?

Zombie: Oh yeah, I forgot.

Chief Inspector: You'll be encouraged to be independent here, you'll attend education as soon as Sergio finds you a tutor. And try out for any jobs he finds you - to see what type of employment would suit you. And we offer hobbies and pastimes to keep you busy. Of course, you will be allowed to have visitors until 11:00 PM and do what you like - within reason in your flat. But you are to keep it tidy and clean and look after it, because budget restrictions mean room maintenance only comes once a week. Right, I'll show you round and once you've settled-in, introduce you to Sergio.

Zombie: Ooh it's got a bedroom, and a bathroom, ooh, and a toilet! is this TV mine? And this table... and this sofa?

Chief Inspector: Yes, everything is yours. But I'll warn you now, any breakages or damage you'll pay for. Sergio will be a lot tougher on you than Sergeant Spicer.

Zombie: Oh baddy baddy.

Chief Inspector: Right, you settle yourself in and I'll bring up Sergio to go over the rules, show you how to budget and take you shopping.

Zombie: What, I'll be in charge of my *own* money and shopping?

Chief Inspector: Yes. But before you say it, you will run out of money pretty soon if you try to buy takeaways all the time. Plus, you'll need to buy your own things like toothpaste, shampoo and loo roll.

Zombie: Boring. Why would I need those anyway??

Chief Inspector: See you in a bit Zombie.

Narrator: Meanwhile, back at the police station, everything is running smoothly, and it is quiet. Very quiet...

Sarge: How's the paperwork going PC Smith?

PC Smith: It's pretty much done Sarge. Surprising how much you can get done without constant interruptions. Do you want a tea when I've done?

Sarge: Yes. And could you put a plastic bag in it when you bring it to me?

PC Smith: A plastic bag Sarge??

Sarge: Yes yes, don't argue.

Narrator: PC Smith finishes up his paperwork and follow Sarge's *unusual* request.

PC Smith: Here's the tea you asked for Sarge.

Sarge: Why is there a plastic bag in my tea PC Smith!

PC Smith: You told me to put a bag in it Sarge.

Sarge: No, no, no PC Smith, when we say bag, we mean TEA bag!

PC Smith: Er… are you alright Sarge…?

Sarge: Oh…er… Yes. Quiet round here, isn't it?

PC Smith: Just as you say you like it, Sarge. Why don't you do some gardening or practise your magic show for this year's festival - now we've got all the paperwork done?

Sarge: Yes, yes, I... think I will. I'll go and talk to my plants.

PC Smith: Oh thank goodness for that, that's the Sarge I know. Thought you'd gone mad for a moment with that tea business. You OK if I pop out to get me and Charlie some tea for tonight?

Sarge: Of course. I'll be in the garden.

Narrator: PC Smith leaves and Sarge talks to his lemon plants...

Sarge: Right, listen up Zombie, you're getting too big for this small pot, I'm going to have to repot you into this bigger pot. *"But Swarge, I like it in this little pot, can I stay please, please, please?"* No Zombie, you heard me. That's an order! *"Right you are Swarge, but can I have a...".* No you can't Zombie, you'll have water - just like the other plants!

Narrator: Zombie has settled into his new place and it's morning. Zombie is getting dressed... or trying to...

Zombie: Sarge, is it two shoes or one shoe? And do they go on the left foot or the right foot? Oh, that's right he's not here... Still, at least I won't have to do my teeth or shower if he's not around. Ooh look, a bit of pizza left on the carpet. Blow the dust off and pop it in my mouth. Ewww, must have been a toenail. Never mind!

Narrator: Just then, there is a knock at the door.

Sergio: Good morning, Zombie. Just doing the morning rounds. When you're dressed and have had breakfast, I expect you in my office to start looking for a job. You'll balance your time between work and education - when we find a tutor. Unless you know of anyone who's happy to do it on a voluntary basis until we can get the funds to pay for them? And one more thing...tidy this room up before you leave, it's a disgrace!

Zombie: Right you are Serge. Serge, how many shoes is it again?

Sergio: One on each foot Zombie. Come on. How did you get dressed before you came here??

Zombie: Sarge used to help me.

Sergio: Well there's gonna be no pussyfooting around here. Understood?

Zombie: Right you are Serge.

Sergio: Good. And one more thing Zombie. Put some underpants on.

Zombie: I have got pants on.

Sergio: Yes... but not on your head, there's a good chap. Goodbye.

Narrator: Zombie somehow manages to get himself dressed when there's another knock at the door. Zombie answers it.

Zombie: What do you want now... oh Zombie 2, what are you doing here??

Zombie 2: I heard you'd moved in, so came to see if I can help you in any way?

Zombie: Well, you could help me clean this place up. Sergio Aguero wants it tidy before I see him about a job. It could do with a good dust.

Zombie 2: Hold on, the last time I helped you do some cleaning, I got into a lot of trouble.

Zombie: Oh yeah, what happened to you about that?

Zombie 2: Well, I got fired at Upper Ringclay and sent here.

Zombie: Oh, that's mean of them.

Zombie 2: Actually, it worked out alright. Turns out it was a film they were shooting, and I walked in during the murder scene. The director thought it was so funny, they decided to keep the scene in the film. It opens at the cinema soon.

Zombie: Ooh, so you're actress now?

Zombie 2: Well, an 'extra'. So why are you here?

Zombie: Oh, nothing much really. Just robbing a post office.

Zombie 2: So, you're a criminal now? I don't think my parents would like me associating with a robber.

Zombie: It's a long story. If you help me clean up here, we can play on my new Xbox later, and I'll tell you then.

Zombie 2: Sounds like a good idea. Let's get started...

Narrator: As they're tidying up, there's another knock at the door...

Zombie: Get that will you 2, I'm tidying the bedroom.

Zombie 2: Will do 1. Hello, can I help you?

Googal: Ooh, so lovely to see you Zombie - you wee joker you. It took me ages to get that miserable git at the police station to tell me where you were.

Zombie 2: I think you want the other Zombie, they're inside. Come in.

Zombie: Googal!

Googal: My mistake wee lassie. If it wasn't for the height difference, the blonde hair and the fact that you are a girl, I would have struggled to tell you apart. Ooh silly me!

Zombie 2: You know each other, do you?

Googal: Aye, we're related.

Zombie 2: How are you related?

Googal: Ooh, I've never been asked that question. You'll have to ask his mother - my sister, to find oot. Sorry. Anyway Zombie, I've called round to see if you want to come and play on the swings?

Zombie: Ooh goody goody. Yes, let's go!

Zombie 2: Haven't we got to see Sergio about a job?

Zombie: Oh yeah, and he'll only moan if we don't go.

Googal: Ooh dear, what will I do now then?

Zombie: You could come with us. He's looking for a tutor. Maybe he'll give *you* the job!

Googal: Ooh yes, and once he's heard me read one of the tales from the Mc Zombie clan, he's bound to give me the job!

Zombie: Well... maybe just see what he's after first... I'll introduce you...

   ... Sergio, this is Googal, you asked me to find you a tutor for you?

Sergio: That's perfect then, because most of the jobs we get; often require two or more people. And I see by the letter your previous employer gave us, it says: Zombie's hard work*ing*. Although the '*ing*' part - is written in different ink... Oh well, maybe his pen ran out. OK, there's a job for two people needed to clean the clock face in town. I'll let them know you're coming. At least that'll be one thing with a clean face, by the end of the day. Hahahaha. Ah, just my little joke. Off you go.

Narrator: The two zombies head off, Sergio has the great fortune of interviewing Googal and, back at the police station, new developments are afoot...

Sarge: So, explain to me again how it works...

PC Smith: OK, so you've heard of social media such as Facebook, Instagram, YouTube and TikTok. Well, we've now got a dedicated police page where we can put out messages and monitor these sites for videos or messages the public post to alert us to any problems, incidents, or goings-on. Think of it like the police scanner radio, but with video and live updates.

Sarge: Putting it that way, it's quite a good idea, I suppose. But what I've read online or seen on YouTube, it's mainly a bunch of self-obsessed people talking drivel or posting cat videos. My daughter is into all of that stuff but give me an old-fashioned pen and paper any day.

PC Smith: Yeah, I agree TikTok crazes are usually stupid people copying other stupid people, but it will be helpful for us.

Sarge: Talking of tock tick or whatever it's called, I haven't heard the village clock strike since this morning, do you think it is broken?

PC Smith: Possibly. I heard it was due for a clean and they're sending someone today to do it. I could look online?

Sarge: You can if you want, but I'm not that interested. I think I'll practise my magic show, now all the paperwork is done. PC Smith, PC Smith...

PC Smith: Yes Sarge?

Sarge: Do you know, there's one thing I can't stand about Salem?

PC Smith: Which is?

Sarge: Exactly!

PC Smith: Eh?? Oh yeah...which is / witches. Oh of course because Salem in America was known for its witches. Very good. Is it OK if I get on with checking our social media pages for any updates?

Sarge: No no that's fine, I'll carry on coming up with jokes for my act. Oh, and see if anything is being reported by the fire brigade, I've just heard an engine go past.

PC Smith: They might be attending *this* incident Sarge...

Narrator: PC Smith shows Sarge a grainy clip of two people see-sawing up and down on the hands of the clock shouting: "Weeee". Then one of them slips but is luckily snagged by their collar and they're left dangling, calling: "Help! Heeelp!"

Sarge: Lucky it was shot from such a distance that you can't identify them then. You'd be embarrassed to say you knew them! No doubt my Neighbourhood Watch chums will tell me about it sometime.

Narrator: The two zombies return to the community and are very pleased with themselves when they report back to Sergio.

Zombie: Aah, we really enjoyed that, didn't we 2? And we got the clock cleaned.

Sergio: Yes… I did get a phone call. But maybe working from heights isn't for you. So tomorrow's job is on the ground. They're digging up the road and will need traffic held up to keep the workmen safe.

Zombie: Ooh, are we going to dig…

Sergio: No, no, no, no…er… you'll be in charge of holding these 'stop' signs and turning them round occasionally.

Zombie: What's it got written on them?

Sergio: Really?? Well, your new tutor will help you there.

Zombie: Googal, you got the job!

Googal: Aye, I'm very persuasive.

Sergio: Persistent! Right, take them back to your flat, so you're ready to go first thing.

Zombie: Will do Serge.

Googal: Aye, but we'll have to do something about those signs, they're all wrong...

Narrator: The next day, Sarge is taking yet another phone call about a traffic jam. This time from Mr. Hill the farmer.

Sarge: ...You're at the front of the queue and have been waiting for 20 minutes? Surely, he's turned the sign round? Oh, he has... But it says 'stop' on the other side!? But he reckons it's different, because it says 'pots', and better than when it was green and said 'og'. OK, I'll send someone round. Goodbye. Right Zombie, I want you to... Oh, I'd better ring Upper Ringclay.

Narrator: The two zombies return very pleased with themselves - oblivious to the chaos they have caused. Sergio is not so pleased...

Sergio: I think your next job ought to be inside. And, as your employer's letter says: you like cake, that works perfectly as the bakery has had their assistant go off sick.

Zombie: Great mistake...

Sergio: What was that Zombie?

Zombie: I said...er... great big cakes. I'll take it.

Narrator: Zombie returns early from his job and he and 2 are eager to get their pay packets.

Sergio: You're back early Zombie.

Zombie: Yeah, we had to shut up early, they ran out of cakes...

Sergio: Looking at the size of you, I can tell why.

Zombie: Well, I might have tried one or two...for quality control purposes. Anyway, hand over the money. Me and 2 want to get on with gaming and a takeaway.

Sergio: OK. Well, this pile - is to pay for damages you've caused to your flat, clock repairs and cakes eaten. And this single note - is what is left of your wages.

Zombie: But that's only enough for one takeaway.

Sergio: Well actually, you ought to spend it on loo roll etc.

Zombie 2:   He doesn't need loo roll, he uses my loo, don't you Zombie?

Zombie: Yeah, but I still have to buy coffee and sugar for every time you come round. I'm gonna tell Saarge.

Sergio: Sarge doesn't run this place, I do. You were told the rules about paying for things. Do you *want* to live here?

Zombie: Yesss. But I didn't think you would really apply the rules!

Sergio: You've got a lot to learn Zombie. I tell you what, if you decorate flat 1 - the tutor's live-in quarters, you can earn your pay back. The janitor was meant to have done it, but I haven't seen him for a while now.

Zombie 2:   Don't say yes Zombie, I've heard it's haunted...

Zombie: R...really? Oh... we'll take Googal with us, since it's gonna be his flat - all the time he is the tutor. Yes, we'll do it Sergio.

Narrator: The two zombies and Googal go to the flat, being very cautious...

Googal: You go first Zombie, since you live around here.

Zombie: I don't want to. There's a wailing noise coming from inside...

Zombie 2: Told you it was haunted.

Narrator: The three carry on arguing until all three fall inside because the door falls off its hinges.

Zombie: Well, we're in now. Oh look, it's got a spotted duvet.

Zombie 2: No, I think that's paint. And look, there's footprints leading up to that wardrobe. But there's no handle to open it.

Narrator: All three prise open the wardrobe to find the janitor inside. In a thick Brummy accent, he says to them:

Gilbert: Thanks guys, three weeks I've been in there fixing that handle to the inside.

Googal: Och, such a clever idea having a handle on the inside - just in case you want to get out.

Zombie 2: But he couldn't get out.

Gilbert: But that wasn't my fault, as soon as I closed the doors it went dark, and I couldn't find the handle again! I'm getting too old for this game. I'm gonna have to have a word with Serge.

Narrator: As time goes by, the two zombies get through as many jobs as takeaways and spend the rest of their time gaming together. Googal settles into his flat, home-tutors the zombies and makes TikTok or YouTube videos if the others are gaming. At the police station, Sarge spends any spare time gardening or perfecting his show and PC Smith prefers to go online.

Sarge: Are you sure you don't want to hear another one of my jokes Smith?

PC Smith: No no, you save them for the show Sarge. Please.

Sarge: Well, look how well my lemon plant is growing.

PC Smith: Wow, that's very impressive I must say. And what's the small one?

Sarge: Oh, that's a lemon too. The one Zombie insisted on looking after.

PC Smith: He didn't do a brilliant job if you ask me.

Sarge: Well as you and I know, if you want to succeed in anything you've got to put in the hard work. Nonetheless, I might offer it to Zombie, if he wants it. Or has the patience to look after it.

PC Smith: Chief Inspector has told us not to really visit to encourage his independence.

Sarge: Yes, I know that, but I might do one of those video calls that you showed me. Let me find his number...

Narrator: Meanwhile, back at Zombie's place, Googal is teaching the two zombies. He's written two words: 'rice' and 'headache' on a board and is asking his class what is written...

Googal: No... No guesses? OK it's Ricky. And to help you remember, it rhymes with sticky as in - sticky rice. Now, what about this next one? Yes, you with your hand up.

Zombie 2: Head lice?

Googal: Ooh very close, no, it's an Italian word headarchie.

Zombie: This is boring. Can you tell us an Onkey and Timmy story?

Googal: Oh OK, you've persuaded me. Close your books and get ready for a tale from the Mc Zombie clan. Onkey upon a Timmy...

Zombie 2: Shouldn't that be 'once upon a time'?

Googal: Don't be daft lassie, if it was **once**, it would begin with a **W**. No, Onkey is Timmy's donkey, and Timmy is carrying him into town to milk him, as his mother has got a headarchie!

Zombie: Hold on Googal, my phone is ringing. It's Sarge! Hello Sarge!

Sarge: Hello Zombie, and Zombie 2.

Zombie: And Googal - look...

Sarge: Oh God, 3 for the price of 1! Hello Googal.

Googal: Hello Sergeant Spice Girl. I hope you're not phoning to take Zombie back; I don't want to have a custody battle.

Sarge: The only custody battle you'll ever be involved in Googal, will be the one that you have over the single braincell you share with your family! Your sister still wearing that saucepan on her head??

Googal: Actually, she's been having therapy. She only wears a frying pan now.

Sarge: Anyway, I was ringing to see if Zombie wanted his lemon plant.

Zombie: Nah, hasn't grown into a lemon yet, so I don't want it.

Googal: I'll take it! If it's free? Yes, I'll grow a great big lemon.

Sarge: That was a fate I was afraid of for my lemon plant...it ending up with a great big lemon! Still, if you want it, pick it up from Mr McGurk's stall at the festival that's coming up.

Googal: Oh I'll be there all right, I was thinking of offering my expertise as a DJ.

Sarge: Oh God really?? And what's your DJ name - MC headed. Hehehehe.

Zombie: Sarge, Sarge, guess what?

Sarge: What?

Zombie: Zombie 2 taught me how to count. Listen... 1, 2...3,4,5, 6, 7...8, 9... 10!

Sarge: That's very good Zombie. Well done 2. But Zombie, why are you now standing on a chair?

Zombie: Just in case you wanted me to count higher!

Sarge: The Lord giveth...and he taketh away. You two look like you could lose some weight though. Judging by the size of you and the empty takeaways strewn around your room!

Googal: Don't you worry about it. I've taken it upon myself to be their personal trainer.

Sarge: Well, you might want to change your shoes.

Googal: Why? I've got two on... and one on each foot as Zombie said.

Sarge: Yes, but one's a welly and the other is a high heel! Anyway, I've got to go. But remember, if you get up to anything, I'll always end up finding out! Bye for now.

Zombie: Bye Sarge. Googal, what's a DJ?

Googal: Och, I'll show you if you come with me to *RadioActive* tonight. It's a club where you write and produce your own songs.

Zombie: Ooh...

Narrator: Googal takes Zombie along and he takes to it like a duck to water. In fact, every spare moment he has, he spends practising from first thing in the morning to last thing at night. Takeaways and gaming have been limited to the weekends and he's even started washing and doing his teeth...certainly when Zombie 2 comes round. (Which are most nights). Googal meanwhile, spends a lot of time making TikTok and YouTube videos.

Googal: Well, hello there viewers, welcome to another instalment from yours truly - the Masked Scotsman. My subscribers will know I haven't posted for a while, since I took the 'bleach-drinking challenge'. But I'm back now, and in today's challenge, I'm going to throw a lit firework down this pipe and sit on it. Wish me luck...

Narrator: The video cuts and fades back in to Googal rubbing his backside...

Googal: Well, hehe, that was a partial success... I suppose. If I can get 1000 *likes* for this video, next week I'll be hitting a grenade with this hammer to see what happens. Of course, safety is always my first priority, so

I'll be doing it indoors away from others. Don't forget to like and subscribe. Bye for noo.

PC Smith: Oh dear, oh dear, that Masked Scotsman is such an idiot, can you believe there are such people in the world Sarge?

Sarge: I'm not interested in all that, what I want to know is where's that piece of paper with all my jokes on? I was sure I put it down near your desk last. Have you seen it?

PC Smith: Er ... No. But why don't you forget about them and use comedy from real life examples. The Masked Scotsman alone, will keep you in material.

Sarge: Well, I might have to if I can't find it. Can you keep looking whilst I answer the phone?

PC Smith: Er... Yeah.

Sarge: Oh Zombie, this is a surprise, what do you want?

Zombie: What do I wear if I'm going to the cinema with someone?

Sarge: A girl, is it? Anyone I know?

Zombie: Never you mind!

Sarge: You're going with Zombie 2 because it's the first showing of the film she's an 'extra' in and you're thinking of going for a meal after, but can't decide whether a curry or Chinese will be best...

Zombie: So, you *do* know who I'm going with!

Sarge: No...yeees. But whether it's as a friend or a date, make sure you've showered and got clean clothes on - and not your Spider-Man outfit. It might be a nice idea to buy her flowers...if it *is* a date.

Zombie: Well, it's not a date! Anyway, where can you get flowers from?

Sarge: Quite a lot of places sell them nowadays. Not from a grave though, do hear Zombie?

Zombie: Right you are Sarge. Bye.

Sarge: He he he.

Narrator: The day of the festival arrives and there's a carnival atmosphere about the place. Even in the police station...

Sarge: I said banana, bicycle, underpants.

PC Smith: You singing MC 2 Chains' song Sarge??

Sarge: Oh, just some nonsense I heard just now on the local radio.

PC Smith: Yeah, that's 2 Chains and the Zombie Collective from *RadioActive*. They're playing today at the festival. Quite a catchy song.

Sarge: I suppose. Anyway, I'm going to have to go with your suggestion and use real life examples for my jokes. And now you've mentioned the Zombie Collective, ideas are flowing to me. He, he, he, he.

PC Smith: Now Upper Ringclay are here, shall we go?

Sarge: Yes.

Narrator: Both arrive at the festival and there's a real party atmosphere...

Chief Inspector: Ah Spicer, Smith. Congratulations on all of your hard work this year, it hasn't gone unnoticed and there's an opening coming up for Inspector I'd like you to consider. That would leave the role of Sergeant free for you Smith. Anyway, I'll leave that with you to think about. Good day.

PC Smith: Well, that is good news. I'm off to find Charlie, do you want me to bring you back a tea Sir?

Sarge: No sod that, I'll have a beer. And Steven, it's Terry.

PC Smith: Right you are...Terry.

Narrator: PC Smith goes off and a familiar face bowls up to Sarge...

Zombie: Sarge!

Sarge: Hello Zombie. Hello 2.

Zombie: Where's PC Smith?

Sarge: He's somewhere around with his partner Charlie.

Zombie: Ooh he's got a girlfriend?

Sarge: Boyfriend.

Zombie: What?? His girlfriend is his boyfriend? But that would be... a man and a man.

Zombie 2: But – we're a zombie and a zombie.

Zombie: Yes we are toozy woozy. Oh, that makes sense now. Are you going to do your magic show?

Sarge: Yes I am, so I don't want you ruining it!

Zombie: I won't, us fellow performers must stick together and support each other. I'm performing with *RadioActive* later.

Sarge: Oh God, you're MC toilet chain!!

Zombie: 2 Chains.

Sarge: And…the Zombie Collective?

Zombie: Yep, that's right - my family. Well, Googal mainly.

Sarge: Dear Lord. I think I'll find out where Smith has got to with that beer! Before I go though, and I'll probably wish I hadn't asked; why are you wearing a blindfold 2??

Zombie 2: Oh, when my parents found out about his past, they said they didn't want me seeing him again.

Sarge: Oh…God. Right, I'm off to meet my daughter and grandson, then get ready for my performance. Enjoy yourselves.

Narrator: Sarge gets his beer, spends time with his daughter and grandson and later, is on stage with his act. Googal and Zombie are at the front watching…

Sarge: Ok, here's another one. Did you hear the one about the daft person who, once they'd learnt how to count, stood on a chair so they could count even higher!

Zombie: Hahahahaha. Ow he's funny my Sarge…

Googal: No he's not, no idiot would do that. I could do better than him. Boo! Boooo!

Zombie: Quiet Googal, I'm trying to listen.

Narrator: But Googal continues interrupting, making comments and heckling – much to the annoyance of the crowd and Zombie.

Googal: Rubbish, I could do better.

Zombie: Googal! You're being embarrassing! I'm off to find 2.

Sarge: And for the end of my show, I need a volunteer to help me with my escapology act…

Googal: I'll help you, but I'll do the escaping from the sack bit, because I'll be much better than you at it. Make way everybody – genius coming through…

Narrator: The crowd laugh and cheer as Googal struggles in the sack, but start to disperse when it is announced that RadioActive are setting up on the main stage…

Zombie: Sarge, have you seen Googal? We're due on stage in a while…not that I really want to see him after him showing me up like that.

Narrator: Sarge points to the sack – and they both laugh.

Googal: Is that you Zombie?

Zombie: No, this is a recording made on a dictaphone – isn't it Sarge?

Sarge: Yes, you have reached the voicemail of Sergeant Spicer – please leave your message after the tone – 'beep'.

Googal: This is a message for Sergeant Spicer – I'm sorry for being rude during your act. I can't get out of this sack, so when you get this message, would you untie me…please?

Narrator: Sarge leaves it a few more minutes, then lets him out so he and Zombie can perform their act…

Zombie's Hard Work – Rap   S1 E12

Compere: Ok everybody, welcome onto the stage MC 2 Chains and the Zombie Collective with their new song.

Zombie: Thank you very much everybody. Without further ado, here is our new song…

My name is Zombie, and this is my tale.

From my creation – right through to jail.

I'm not very bright – only know three words.

I leave all that learning up to the nerds.

But if you get stuck and don't know what to say,

I'll tell you my words, and these are they:

Banana, bicycle, underpants.

I said: banana, bicycle, underpants.

Now if you know more, good for you,

But I being me find three will do!

So, when I met Sarge, he wasn't impressed,

He had to brush my teeth and get me dressed.

When I'm around he gets uptight

He stops me eating crayons and swinging on the light.

[you know what I say to him...]

Banana, bicycle, underpants.

I said: banana, bicycle, underpants.

Me and PC Smith have to make Sarge tea.

With the amount he drinks, he's bound to need a

Wee sit down and take the weight off his feet.

But no, not Sarge – he takes me on his beat.

We go past the butcher's and past the baker.

Ooh there's a park (I'll visit that later!)

[but for now]

Banana, bicycle, underpants.

I said: banana, bicycle, underpants.

Then there's McGurk – who's as blind as a bat.

If he saw a dinosaur, he'd call it a cat!

[here kitty kitty]

Now Mrs. McGurk, she's a different matter.

She stands in her allotment – and boy can she natter.

[she's no push-over though...sorry Mrs. McGurk]

And Mr. Hill the farmer is the cream of the crop.

But he'll get irate if the sign says STOP.

Banana, bicycle, underpants.

I said: banana, bicycle, underpants.

Now Sarge's daughter I think is great.

But don't start thinking you can take her on a date!

They took me on holiday in the back of their car.

By the time they discovered me – they'd got too far.

I also hid my family right at the back.

Sarge wasn't pleased but we enjoyed the craic.

[I tell you what he didn't say]

Banana, bicycle, underpants.

I said: banana, bicycle, underpants.

[Tell 'em about our family Googal]

Well my name is Googal, I'm a a bit of a 'noodle'.

People say my brain is the size of a poodle's.

His mum likes to wear a pan on her head.

From when she wakes up to when she goes to bed.

And the twins and Granny, often delight us.

But whatever you do – don't mention arthritis.

Banana, bicycle, underpants.

I said: banana, bicycle, underpants.

[go on Sarge, your go]

They call me Sarge, but I'm Terry Spicer.

And if it wasn't for criminals – I'd be much nicer.
And to those 'wrong'uns' who make our life hell.
Step right this way... to my nice prison cell!
But I won't beat you to make you confess.
I'll chuck in Zombie – and he'll do the rest.

Banana, bicycle, underpants.
I said: banana, bicycle, underpants.

Yeah, Sarge is right, I do have that knack.
And up until recently, my life was on track.
I've had some knocks (and cake!) on the way.
And without my hard work, I would have gone astray.
But now I'm sorted (well, over the worst).
So, I'll leave you all with this final verse -
Banana, bicycle, underpants.
I said: banana, bicycle, underpants.

Narrator: The crowd cheer and clap and when Zombie and the Zombie Collective end their show – fireworks are set off...

Printed in Great Britain
by Amazon